A GRAVE GIRLS' GETAWAY

A NIGHT HUNTRESS NOVELLA

JEANIENE FROST

This ebook is licensed to you for your personal enjoyment only.

This is a work of fiction. Names, characters, places, and incidents are either products of the writer's imagination or are used fictitiously and are not to be construed as real. Any resemblance to actual events, locales, organizations, or persons, living or dead, is entirely coincidental.

"A Grave Girls Getaway." Originally published in *Hex on the Beach*. Copyright © 2021 by Jeaniene Frost.

Ebook ISBN: 9781641972161

Print KDP ISBN: 9798784180834

Print IS ISBN: 9781641971935

ALL RIGHTS RESERVED.

No part of this work may be used, reproduced, or transmitted in any form or by any means, electronic or mechanical, without prior permission in writing from the publisher, except in the case of brief quotations embodied in critical articles or reviews.

NYLA Publishing

121 W 27th St., Suite 1201, New York, NY 10001

http://www.nyliterary.com

CHAPTER 1

I was *not* spying on my daughter. I wasn't.

Sure, I was flying to the spot in the woods where Katie was, but that wasn't to avoid her hearing my footsteps. It was just…convenience. If you came from a line of flight-capable Master vamps like I did, would you dirty your shoes by trudging through the dirt and leaves?

And sure, I was avoiding branches that would snap in a telltale way if I got too close, but that didn't prove anything. Why ruin the natural sounds of the forest?

Okay, fine, my slowing down and ducking behind a tree when I glimpsed Katie was incriminating, but why couldn't a mother enjoy a few private moments admiring her recently discovered daughter? Katie was lovely, with auburn-colored hair, the same dark gray eyes as mine, skin like sunlight on snow, and an uncommon gracefulness that was on full display as she danced among the trees.

If I still breathed, my breath would have caught as I watched her. I'd had her in my life less than three years, so I didn't have the memories most parents had of watching their babies coo in the crib, or laugh for the first time, or take their first steps, but I could watch Katie dance now, and it was indescribably beautiful. No prima ballerina had Katie's grace, precision, or speed.

And that was why we still had to keep her hidden. Those traits would reveal that Katie wasn't fully human. Mixed species people might be legal now, but Katie's particular blend of species had almost caused two undead wars before.

I was about to call out to her when she suddenly turned a pirouette into a roundhouse kick that leveled a nearby birch tree. Another spinning combination took out a larger spruce to her left, and then a ferocious roll-and-kick combo felled three evergreens in a row. As the coup de grâce, she ripped the stump of the nearest toppled evergreen out of the ground, and then held it up by its roots as if the stump were a decapitated head.

Dammit! Katie wasn't out here secretly dancing. She was practicing killing. Again.

I knew something was up with all her recent "walks." That's why I was spying on her—and yes, I had known all along that I was spying. Don't judge; motherhood was still very new and overwhelming to me. Hell, I hadn't even known I was a mother until a few years ago, when I found out that—while I was unconscious—my eggs had been harvested, fertilized, and implanted into a surrogate. Sound impossible? So does a half-vampire working for a secret branch of Homeland Security that polices murderously misbehaving members of the undead society, but that was my old job. Unbeknownst to me, I'd also been a guinea pig for a shadowy government official who'd been trying to create a paranormal super soldier. He'd succeeded with Katie, and though she was only ten years old, all the growth hormones they'd pumped into her meant that she looked several years older. The worst part, though, was by the time I found her she'd already racked up a body count that would do a hardened mercenary proud.

I'd spent the last few years trying to undo the brutal tutelage Katie had received when she was the government's secret weapon, hoping that with time, she would forget much of her early years. My husband, Bones, and I had given Katie as normal a life as we could, especially considering that we were both vampires hiding out from the vampire world because of Katie's unique combination of species.

We thought we'd been making progress with Katie, yet here she was practicing killing people again despite being told that killing was wrong. Did she think I couldn't protect her? Or did… did she *miss* killing people?

If she were human, I could read her mind and know the answer, but Katie was inhuman enough for her thoughts to be locked away. That left me guessing, and I couldn't come up with any innocent reason for what she was doing. Despair pricked me. Maybe I hadn't given Katie enough normal to help undo the massive psychological damage done to her. Was that why she was reverting back to her old behaviors?

My lips tightened as I shoved my despair aside. If my daughter needed more normal in order to break free from her horrifying past, then fine. I'd deliver an ass-ton of it.

Later, I gripped my knife so hard that my knuckles whitened. I'd been in many battles before, but seldom had my nerves been stretched this tight.

"You'd better be worth it," I said to my prey.

One hard slice later, my hopes shattered. "Mother…fudger!" I swore, altering the curse just in time.

A stifled laugh behind me increased my ire. I whirled to see my mother turning away with her hand covering her traitorously twitching lips.

"I told you to take the turkey out half an hour ago," Justina murmured.

Yes, well, the meat thermometer hadn't registered 165 degrees then, and the recipe said poultry *had* to be cooked to at least 165 degrees. I gave the meat thermometer an evil look. Either it was broken, or it was possessed by the spirit of a vengeful chef bent on destroying my attempts at a nice family dinner. Hey, stranger things had happened.

"Sorry. Dinner's going to suck, but on the bright side, no one's getting salmonella from *this* burnt offering."

"You're all vampires, and I'm not fully human, so salmonella can't harm any of us," Katie replied. Her tone was faintly quizzical, as if she was trying to hide her surprise that I hadn't figured that out for myself.

"I know, honey," I said gently. "I was making a joke."

"Ah," she said. Then, she smiled a little too wide. "Of course. Your joke was very entertaining!"

Now I was the one smiling. Despite Katie's many skills, she had yet to master lying. It was almost comforting.

"Don't fret," Bones replied, getting up and moving into the kitchen. "That bird will do nicely with the right roux. Give me a few minutes, Kitten."

I left the kitchen, defeated by it once again. No matter how many recipes I tried, I still couldn't cook to save my life.

Bones began whisking the pan drippings while adding wine, spices, flour, and other ingredients. Soon, the aroma was heavenly. His roux, or gravy, as we Americans called it, was so good that it made even the overcooked turkey delicious.

By the end of dinner, I would have called tonight a success, except for what Katie said after taking her plate to the sink: "I'm going for a walk in the woods."

Granted, ten o'clock at night might be well past bedtime for a human child, but for a household of vampires, it was barely evening. Also, our nearest neighbor was several acres away in this stretch of forested land in Mission, British Columbia, Canada, so she was safe. Still, I tensed.

Going for a walk, my ass!
I had to handle this. I just wasn't sure how to do so yet.
"Fine, but don't be gone too long."

CHAPTER 2

I waited until I couldn't hear Katie's footsteps anymore before I said, "She's up to no good out there."

My mother's eyes widened. "She isn't smoking, is she?"

"I wish," I replied with feeling.

Justina gave me an appalled glance. My wave dismissed it.

"That would at least be an expected form of pre-teen rebellion. She's sneaking off to practice killing."

Saying it out loud made it more real. Guilt, grief, and rage scalded me with its usual toxic mixture. I saved Katie from the human monsters that had held her captive, so why couldn't I save her from the horrible things she'd learned from them?

"You've been spying on her?" Bones sounded more surprised by that than he was by hearing of Katie's activities.

"I prefer 'practicing attentive parenting,'" I muttered.

His look plainly said, *Who are you bullshitting?*

I threw up my hands. "Fine! Spying on her is messed up, but that's hardly our main concern, is it?"

"Kitten, we told Katie it was wrong to kill anyone who wasn't trying to harm her, but we never told her that she couldn't still train."

My eyes widened. "Isn't that focusing on the letter of the law while ignoring the *intent*?"

"Maybe training is just familiar to her?" my mother said.

Justina, the excuse-making, indulgent grandmother? Never would've pegged her for that, but here she was, showing Katie more understanding for her trial slaughters than she'd shown me my entire childhood.

"She wasn't just shadowboxing, Mom. She was kicking trees in half and then decapitating their fallen stumps."

And appearing to enjoy it. That worried me the most. Had she *enjoyed* killing people in her former life?

Bones didn't look concerned. For a second, something flashed across his face that looked traitorously like approval.

"Oh, come on," I snapped. "She's just a child!"

His dark brown eyes seemed to stare into my soul. "Yes, but she's no ordinary child, and you know it. So, what's really bothering you about this, Kitten?"

"I keep screwing things up with her!"

The words burst from me while emotions that I tried not to think about, let alone show, exploded free like a cork shooting out of a shaken-up champagne bottle.

"I wasn't there for the first seven years of her life when she was experimented on and forced into becoming a killer," I said, trying to regain control. "Now? What sort of mother am I? I can't cook, I keep dropping f-bombs, I could barely stitch the tear in her favorite pants, and, oh yeah, I'm spying on her."

My mother stood, not appearing to notice that she upended her chair with her fast, jerky movements.

"You love your daughter as she is." Her voice vibrated, and I was shocked to see her eyes shine with unshed tears. I could count on one hand the number of times I'd seen my mother cry.

"I failed to do that with you when you were growing up, and it almost killed you. Don't worry about the other stuff. Keep loving your daughter unconditionally, Catherine, and unlike me, you'll always be a *wonderful* mother."

With that, she left. Moments later, I heard her car start, and then the spin of gravel as she pulled away.

"Your mum is right."

Bones's statement broke the silence. I turned toward him, a humorless smile tugging my mouth.

"You and my mom agreeing? Is it the apocalypse again?"

He smiled back although his gaze was serious. "Hope not, but still, she's right. You'd see it, too, if you weren't so busy punishing yourself for what happened to Katie before we found her."

Damn Bones. He always cut to the heart of matters, and worse, he frequently used logic as his scalpel.

"I know I'm not responsible for what was done to Katie, but I *feel* like I am," I admitted. "Maybe, deep down, Katie feels that way, too? Maybe that's why she's acting out this way?"

Bones let out a soft snort. "Kitten, Katie isn't doing this because she blames you for what happened to her."

"Why, then?"

Bones gave me an unfathomable look. "Ask her, but not now. Ask her after you've had a mental break from trying to make up for every evil deed that someone else committed against her. That way, you'll be able to truly hear her answer."

"How do you propose I get this cleansing mental break?" I said with a wry scoff. "Give myself a lobotomy?"

His lip curled. "Those don't work on vampires, so we'll go with the more effective option of going on a getaway."

I waited, but he didn't follow up with 'just kidding!' "You think I'll stop worrying about Katie if we're off somewhere where neither of us can make sure that she's okay?"

"'Course not," he replied in an easygoing tone. "That's why I'll be staying behind, and you'll go."

I laughed. He only arched a brow.

"I'm quite serious. Denise was just saying it's been too long since she's seen you. I'm sure she'd love the chance to catch up, and Charles can certainly spare her for a week."

Charles was Bones's best friend, just like Denise was mine. I hadn't seen her in several months, and I missed her, but...

"I can't just up and leave. Katie—"

"We will be fine," Bones interrupted. "I'll be here, your mum and Tate are right down the road, and your uncle still floats by frequently though the spectral sod thinks I don't know it."

"That sounds great, but...uh..."

"Can't imagine doing something solely for yourself?" Bones let out a knowing grunt. "Like most good mums, you're too focused on everyone else, and now you're burnt out from taking on too much. Time to recharge, luv. You deserve it. I'll miss you, but we both know you won't relax unless I'm here with Katie, so ring Denise and tell her you're inviting her to a girls-only getaway. She'll love it."

I had no doubt. I kind of loved it, too, even if I had already started to think of a hundred reasons why I shouldn't do it. Still, I hadn't had a vacation in...God, several years.

"Fine. I'll call Denise."

"Call her later. Now, we're making the most of Katie being out of the house. Have to give you a good reason to miss me, don't I?"

He gave me a heated glance while a far hotter emotion slid through my subconscious, suffusing me with tantalizing sensations. He'd changed me into a full vampire, and that bond meant I felt his emotions as if they were my own—if he wanted me to. He wanted me to now, and when he grabbed me, his low laugh teased my lips before his mouth covered mine.

I barely noticed the blur of household fixtures as Bones flew us out of the kitchen and up the stairs. When we reached our bedroom, the door closed behind us on its own, and my clothes came off without either of us touching them.

Cooking wasn't the only thing Bones excelled at. He'd also become a fairly powerful telekinetic, and he'd expanded his abilities far beyond moving simple objects with his mind. My moan turned into a gasp as both his hands and his power slid over me, caressing and teasing with knowing, skillful touches. Then my gasps turned into cries when his mouth replaced his hands, and his tongue shot honeyed fire through my veins.

I writhed beneath him, too caught up to say more than a panted "Now!" as I tried to pull him up from between my thighs.

His laugh hit my flesh like an erotic brush of feathers.

"Not yet, Kitten. I did say you needed some 'you' time, didn't I? Let me get back to work on that…"

CHAPTER 3

*B*y the time I left on my trip, I was feeling far less guilty. Katie seemed to look forward to having some one-on-one time with Bones. In fact, they'd both all but shoved me out the door. I mused on that as I waited for Denise. Maybe in my attempt to be an attentive mom, I'd been smothering Katie? How did anyone manage to raise a kid without constantly screwing up?

"Cat!"

I turned to see a beautiful woman with long, mahogany-colored hair and hazel eyes running across the hotel lobby toward me. I barely had a second to brace myself before Denise launched herself at me. Her momentum swung us in a circle, and I found myself breathing in her familiar scent of honey and jasmine as I hugged her back.

She caught what I was doing and laughed. "You're smelling me, aren't you?"

I grinned, sheepish. "Sorry, but hey, at least I didn't give you an exploratory bite, too."

She snorted. "I'm not your brand, remember?"

No, she wasn't. Because of my funky half-breed lineage, I was the only vampire who didn't drink human blood. Instead, I fed from other vampires, not that most of my kind knew that. That's why I had a couple bags of Bones's blood packed in with my clothes. Sure, I could eat real food, but it didn't nourish or strengthen me the way vampire blood did.

Denise gave me a wide grin. "I'm so glad you're really here! I kept thinking some emergency would make you cancel."

I fought a wince. I'd cancelled lots of plans with her in the past several years. Guess that made me a bad friend in addition to my questionable mothering abilities. In my defense, someone had usually been trying to kill me during all the times I'd cancelled. Fighting off an attempted murderer was hardly a "the more, the merrier!" type of occasion.

"Nope. I'm here, and we're going to have so much fun."

"You bet, and look at this place!"

She waved at the sumptuous lobby, where the huge domed ceiling hung like a crown over the ornately designed floor. All that paled next to the magnificent views of the Pacific Ocean through the many windows. The Ritz Carlton at Half Moon Bay sprawled on top of steep bluffs like a modern version of a medieval castle. Only a narrow strip of beach ran between those bluffs and the surf, and further up that sandy stretch, there were tide pools that would soon be swallowed up by the incoming high tide.

"The ocean in front of us, and redwood forests behind us," Denise continued. "Plus, the clubs in San Francisco are only half an hour away. This is perfect! I wasn't expecting this, to be honest." She paused to grin again when I squirmed, and then teased, "Bones picked this place out, didn't he?"

Denise knew my thriftiness would never allow me to splurge like this, even if I thought it was perfect, too.

"Of course he did."

She laughed. "I'll compliment him on his taste later. Now, let's get dressed in something fabulous. Tomorrow, we're hiking in the redwoods or going horseback riding on the beach, but tonight, we're shutting down the clubs."

I couldn't remember the last time I'd gone to a club just to have fun. Mostly, I went clubbing to hunt and kill vampires. Tonight, though, all I'd be a danger to were gin and tonics.

"Sounds great, and if you like this, wait until you see our rooms. We have our own mini cottage on the beach."

Denise groaned in mock ecstasy. I grinned as I made a mental note to call Bones later and thank him. Maybe he was right, and this break was just what I needed. I already felt better, and the night hadn't even begun yet.

SEVERAL HOURS LATER, Denise and I walked down the beach, both of us holding our shoes instead of wearing them. The foamy surf came closer, threatening to soak our feet. Our hotel was still a few miles ahead, but we'd chosen to walk since it was such a lovely night. Still, the incoming tide might force us to change that plan.

It wouldn't be the first time we'd changed our plans tonight. So much for shutting down the clubs. We hadn't even lasted until midnight before both of us decided to head back. Even now, Denise shook her head, bemused.

"Were clubs always that loud? I could hardly hear a word you said, and damn, were we the only ones *not* high? I swear, I saw twenty pill handoffs at that last place, and some of those kids looked like teenagers!"

I let out an amused sniff. "They weren't. They only looked that young because we're getting older."

"Thirties is *not* old," she said at once.

"Of course it isn't, but it's old enough to admit when we're not having a good time versus staying and faking it."

She shook her head. "I don't get it. I used to love dancing all night. Now? My feet hurt, my ears are ringing, and I want to curl up on the couch and order dessert from room service."

I laughed. "That sounds great to me, too."

Denise gave me a wry grin. "I'm still kinda human, but you're a vampire. What's your excuse for crapping out early?"

"Spending time with you," I replied. "Like you said, it was too loud to talk before, and I've missed you."

"I've missed you, too."

We kept walking, chatting with an openness we hadn't managed in a while. Calls, texts, and video chats were great, but they didn't beat the joy of being together.

Soon, we reached what was left of the tide pools. I slowed my stride to avoid slipping, and then caught Denise's shoulder when she almost stumbled on the uneven rock.

"Want to head back to the street and call a Lyft?" I asked.

"Or you could fly us over these," she pointed out.

I could, but vampires had kept their existence hidden from humanity because we avoided public displays of power. Still, it was pitch dark, and the nearest hotel was a good mile away. I sent my senses outward. Nope, I didn't hear anyone else along the beach…Wait. I strained my senses more.

There. Someone was in the caves tucked into the bluffs bordering the beach and the sea. If I were human, I wouldn't have heard the low murmur of voices that almost blended with the sounds of the surf, and I *really* wouldn't have caught the new tang to the air before the sea spray snatched it away.

Still, that brief, sharp, new scent was unmistakable, *especially* to a vampire.

Blood.

"Earth to Cat," Denise began.

I pressed a finger to my lips in the universal gesture for silence. Then, I leaned in and whispered, "Stay here. Something's wrong," against her ear.

Maybe that blood was from a normal crime, or maybe I wasn't the only person out here with supernaturally great hearing.

I flew toward the sounds and the smell of blood.

At first, I was confused when I reached the spot where the

scent and sounds were strongest. Nothing but smooth, unbroken cliff wall met my gaze. Where was the entrance? There had to be one, and…what was that? A new, stronger wave had swept seawater all the way up to the cliff. It stopped everywhere except in one spot, where the water somehow disappeared into the rock.

I tried to touch that spot, and like the water, my hand vanished as it appeared to go through the wall of stone. I pulled it out and did it again. Same result, only this time, I concentrated and felt cool air coming from the side where I could no longer see my hand.

This part of the wall wasn't real. It was glamour, the term for a magical mirage. To use this, someone really didn't want their bloodletting interrupted.

Too bad.

I felt around until I found the rest of the entrance. Then, I squeezed into the hidden cave. Once inside, the glamour disappeared, revealing a narrow passageway. The smell of blood pointed my way, as did the sounds that I realized were chants in an unfamiliar language. Now, I caught snatches of thoughts, too.

…can't be happening…oh God, no…no, please, stop!

Chanting, pleas, magic, and blood—never a good combination.

I kept going, ducking when a new, flickering light appeared after a sharp bend in the tunnel. I could pick out several voices from the chants, and underneath them, the ominous sounds of grunts, as if someone was trying to scream and couldn't.

I pulled a knife from its sheath beneath my skirt. Since I found out at sixteen that silver through the heart killed vampires, I'd never left home without one. I'd barely palmed the silver blade when icy water soaked me to the ankles.

The incoming tide had reached the cave. This whole place would be underwater soon. I might be beyond drowning, but whoever was bleeding wasn't.

Fuck being stealthy. It wasn't my style, anyway.

"Housekeeping!" I sang out, and flew around the corner.

Nine hooded heads jerked up. The robed figures all appeared to be women, and four of them were vampires. Weak ones, if their auras could be trusted. Must be why I hadn't felt their energy before now. Strong vampires usually gave off vibes like an electrical current.

"Get out," a vampire with hair as red as my own snapped.

Torchlight revealed runes and other ancient markings drawn onto the cave walls. The women were standing around a pentagram that had a gagged, panicked boy inside it. He couldn't have been more than seventeen, and runes had been carved onto his chest, leaving bloody trails running down his body. No surprise, the mental pleas I'd overhead were coming from him.

"Hell no," I said, pissed for more reasons than their clear intention to murder this kid. "Less than a year after magic's been declared legal, you bitches are doing a ritual sacrifice of a teenager? First, that's evil, and second, are you *trying* to give the vampire council a reason to ban magic again? Innocent witches did not fight so hard for freedom from persecution for you selfish schmucks to fuck it up this way!"

The redhead wasn't the only one giving me an incredulous look. Guess the last thing they expected was a lecture, but magic wasn't the only thing that the vampire council had recently declared to be legal. Mixed species people like Katie were now legal, too, and it wasn't a stretch to assume that if one law got overturned because of assholes like these witches, the other law would get overturned, too.

"We obey no earthly council," the redheaded vampire hissed. "And you have sealed your fate, intruder. Now, we will have two sacrifices to give our goddess instead of one."

Oh, she'd picked the wrong girl on the wrong night. Anticipation thrummed through me. Hiding with Katie had retired me from my former ass-kicking lifestyle, and I hadn't realized how much I missed it until now.

More water rushed around my ankles. It was now up to the

bloody boy's cheek since they had him restrained to the cave floor. He flailed, the stench of his fear almost choking.

Don't worry, kid. You're not dying on my watch.

I snapped his restraints with a single, concentrated thought. One perk of being a freaky vampire who fed from other vampires was that I temporarily absorbed any powers the other vampire had. Bones was my favorite food, and since he was telekinetic, I had some of that power, too. I wasn't nearly as good at it as he was, but small, inanimate objects were easy.

"What?" the redheaded leader said in shock.

I gave her a nasty smile. "Yeah, and that's not all I've got."

CHAPTER 4

Silver flashed in their hands as her three vampire minions lunged at me. I flew straight up, causing them to smack into each other instead of me. Then, I flung my silver knife.

It landed in the blonde vampire's heart. With another concentrated thought, I gave it a hard twist while using my body's downward momentum to slam the other two vampires against the cave walls. One vampire's head hit the wall so hard that she instantly went down, but the black-haired one screamed as she raised her knife and aimed for my unprotected back.

With a focused thought, I yanked the knife from her hand and sent it into her chest with another hard twist. Now two of the vampires were dead.

This was too easy. If they hadn't been about to murder a teenager, I might've felt bad about slaughtering them this way.

"Stop!"

I whirled to see that the redheaded witch now had the boy up against her chest while her back was to the cave's wall. Smart. Now her heart was protected from both sides. She also had an ancient-looking knife pressed against his throat, and her eyes glowed with a vampire's trademark bright emerald light.

"One more move and he dies," she swore.

"Hurt him and I'll rip your head off right now," I countered.

Her smile showed her newly extended fangs. "No, you won't. If your powers were that great, I'd already be dead."

Ooh, a thinker. She was right, too. I hadn't mastered the ability to use my borrowed telekinesis on people yet, especially people with supernatural energy like vampires. But I didn't need to be able to control her to stop her.

I focused on her knife, and then yanked with all the mental strength I had. To my shock, the blade didn't even budge.

If snakes could grin, their smiles would look just like the one the redhead flashed me. "Your impressive abilities are useless against enchanted objects, intruder."

Inwardly, I cursed, but all I said was, "Really? Guess life's a bitch until one kills you."

"You *will* die," she said flatly. "Pity. With your abilities, you would have been an asset to our coven."

Her human acolytes started to chant in the strange language again. From their thoughts, this spell would end with my death. So much for thinking this was too easy. I'd seen how nasty magic could get in the hands of a skilled practitioner, and if the redhead had an enchanted weapon, she wasn't a poser or an amateur.

That's why I couldn't let her minions finish their incantation. The humans might be easy to incapacitate, but if I went for the last two vampires, I risked the boy's life. How to stop the chants without endangering him?

I glanced above the redhead. Yes. That could work.

I put my hands up in an "I surrender" pose. "Maybe we can come to an agreement—"

The redhead's scoff cut me off. "After you killed two members of my coven? Our only agreement is your death."

I readied my power, careful to look only at her. "You don't want to do that."

She scoffed again. "Oh, but I do."

Just a few moments more... "Not if you don't want a shitload of trouble. I'm Cat Crawfield Russell, and if you don't know that name, does the term 'Red Reaper' ring a bell?"

From her widened gaze, it did. "Wife of Bones, and friend of Vlad Dracul," she whispered.

I'd earned my nickname after cutting a bloody swath through the undead world when I was still half human, and she was defining me only by my relationships with the *men* in my life?

"You don't deserve a vagina," I muttered, and finished wrapping my power around the thin slice of protruding rock above her. With a mental yank, I tore the rock free.

The narrow slice of ledge slammed into her hard enough to take off her head. I lunged at the same moment, pulling the boy down so he was out of the rock's deadly, slicing path. Then, I took advantage of the other witches' shock to rip my knife through the nearest one's heart.

My head exploded with pain. I turned, seeing the formerly unconscious vampire through a haze of red as blood dripped into my eyes. At some point during my exchange with her leader, she'd woken up. Now, she held a piece of debris in her hands, its tip stained with scarlet. I was so dazed that it took a second to figure out what it was.

Bitch had brained me with the rock ledge I'd just used to kill her coven leader. Admirable, really.

I ducked under her next swing and managed a sideways kick that knocked her briefly unconscious again. I tried to use my abilities to send a silver knife flying into her heart, but though I concentrated, nothing happened. Guess the decent-sized piece of my skull on the ground meant my telekinesis was temporarily out of order.

The boy stared at me in horror.

"Run!" I said, fumbling around to grab one of the silver knives from the dead vampires.

He did, and after my second try, I had a knife. My head felt a little better, too. God bless vampire healing abilities.

Problem was, I wasn't the only one healing. The final vampire jumped up, giving me an evil glare. She didn't lunge at me, though. She stayed back, making me come to her.

I did until my legs suddenly had trouble working. *What the hell?* She'd whacked my head before, not my legs...

The spell, I realized. Shit. Not amateurs *at all.*

I changed course and flew at the chanting witches. This area of the cave was so small, it didn't matter that my power failed halfway through my flight. I still barreled into them, slashing as I went. Blood coated me in a hot spray, and two of the human witches fell. What I'd lacked in coordination, I'd made up for in strength. The other two witches screamed as their friend's head bobbed up and down in the water next to them.

Then they ran. Or tried to. The seawater hampered their strides since it was now up to our waists.

But one of the running witches was still chanting, and pain blasted through me as the remaining vampire slammed my head against the cave wall. I tried to block her next blow but ended up only swatting at her hands. *Damn that spell!* I felt like I'd been dropped into a cylinder of quick-dry cement.

The witch's chant grew until she was screaming. My vampire attacker smirked as my legs suddenly couldn't hold me up. Water went over my head as I collapsed beneath the waves and the weight of the spell. Through the haze of the sea, I saw the vampire walk away, presumably to fetch a silver knife. If vampire bodies floated, she'd have her pick of knives from the ones sticking out of her dead friends, but vampires lacked air in our lungs, so her dead friends had sunk straight to the cave's bottom. Just like I had.

I tried to force my body free of the invisible hold over it. Nothing happened, not even a twitch. *Fucking hell!* Why hadn't I learned any defensive magic? I'd learned every which way to fight, but only physically. Not mystically.

The vampire hauled me up from the water so I could see her smile as she raised a silver knife. For some reason, I found myself taking in every detail of her appearance. Cornsilk blonde hair, sky-blue eyes, skin as pale as a porcelain doll, and a near flawless complexion, except for a little scar near her eyebrow that she must have gotten when she was human.

Was this what people who were about to die did? Memorize the last face they saw, even if that face belonged to their killer?

Anger surged, so hot and fierce, I half expected the water around me to start boiling. Fuck her, I was *not* going to die this way! I might not be able to move, and my borrowed telekinetic powers might not work on vampires, but I wasn't totally helpless. She still needed that knife to kill me.

I focused on it with everything I had. Just as she slammed the blade home, it shattered into a thousand pieces, leaving only her hand to hit my chest. She stared at it in disbelief, and then stared at the roiling water that swallowed up the now-tiny silver shards that used to be the knife.

I kept my mind wrapped around a few of those shards as the vampire screamed and began bashing my head against the cave wall. Guess she'd decided on decapitation by battery since she could no longer stab me to death.

My vision went red, and not in a rage sort of way. In the *oh shit, I have massive cranial hemorrhaging* way. Acid being poured into my brain likely would've hurt less, and I could do nothing to defend myself. I only had one shot to survive, so I used the last of my quickly fading mental power to form those silver shards into a long point.

Then, right as an ominous ringing overshadowed the sickening crash-crunch-repeat sounds of my head being pulverized, I sent the combined shards toward her heart and twisted.

The next instant, everything went dark.

CHAPTER 5

Ow.

No, really, *owwww!* If anything hurt more than a mostly-shattered head knitting itself back together, I hadn't felt it yet. I puked three times inside my mouth before I had enough coherence to try spitting it out, and then I was frustrated and furious when I couldn't move enough to do that.

Damn that spell! No wonder some vampires had been so afraid of magic that they'd convinced the ruling council to outlaw it for thousands of years. I was normally strong enough to bench press a car, and now I couldn't so much as spit.

But, spitless or no, and collapsed in an underwater cave or no, I was still alive. *Thank you, freaky power-absorbing abilities. I couldn't have done this without you.*

Something hard hit me, interrupting my gratitude. Great, was it the final vampire? I thought I'd twisted that blade and killed her, but maybe I hadn't. Everything had gone black before I could be sure she was dead.

Another hard thump, and then I felt a leg. A warm one.

Not the vampire then. Our species was room temperature, and

in this cold water, we'd feel downright chilly. Whoever this leg belonged to was human.

Was it the boy? I'd told him to run, dammit. Or was it the final chanting witch? I hadn't heard her during those last moments before I passed out, but that didn't mean it was because she'd left the cave. More likely, it was because I couldn't hear anything beyond my skull being beaten in.

If it was her, she could be trying to finish me off. Normally, a human wouldn't stand a chance against a vampire, but in my condition, she'd have reason to feel confident.

Whoever it was yanked on my arm. I tried to shake off the mental fog that made me feel like cotton had replaced my brain.

Focus, Cat! You probably have to mind-smash one more knife!

She yanked harder, and my head cleared the surface. The first thing I saw was mahogany-colored hair plastered to a familiar face before that face broke into a smile.

"Thank God, I found you!"

I was shocked. What was Denise doing here? The water was so high, she barely had any room to breathe.

"Are you hurt? Why aren't you moving?" she asked me.

I couldn't answer, of course. I could only stare at her.

"What's wrong with you?" Now she sounded scared.

She should be. I found that I could move my eyes, and I glanced at the ceiling, the water level only inches below it, and back at her.

Get it, Denise? You're the one in danger!

"Yeah, I know," she muttered, and then relief suffused her features. "If you can manage to show your annoyance despite not being able to move or speak, then you're still in there. Good. I was afraid you might be dead."

She'd been married to a vampire for years; didn't she remember that we shriveled back to our true age when we bit the dust? Some vamps looked like old-school mummies after they died. Then again, I hadn't been changed into a full vampire that long ago, so I guess Denise had had reason to be unsure.

"Gotta get out of here, but I don't have your vision, and the torches are all out," she said, more to herself than me.

She was right. It was almost pitch-black in here, and with the cave's bends and turns now hidden underwater, it would be easy to get lost. And trapped. At least the part of Denise that wasn't human protected her from all but one form of death, and drowning wasn't it.

Still, drowning and coming back only to drown again and again would be horrible until low tide came and took the water away. Besides, who's to say the two witches who'd escaped wouldn't be back with reinforcements before then?

"Do your eyes still work?" Denise suddenly asked.

What did she mean by…? Oh, right.

I let out the green glow in my gaze. An emerald light instantly illuminated a couple feet of the cave. Denise gave the light a critical look, and then hefted me over her shoulders.

"Ugh, you're really heavy."

There goes your Hanukkah present, I thought irreverently.

"This isn't going to work," she said after dragging me a few feet. "The water's hampering me, and you're dead weight."

Go, I tried to tell her with my gaze.

She'd done everything she could. I'd have to wait for the spell to wear off.

Denise glanced up again. The ceiling was now brushing the top of her head. Soon, there wouldn't be enough room for her to breathe at all. She barely had time to get herself out of the cave even if she left me right now.

Go! I thought again, my gaze brightening with urgency.

A look of obstinance crossed her features, and she hauled my face close to hers. "I know what you're thinking, and no, I'm not leaving you behind. You'd never do that to me—"

A new surge from the tide swept water into her mouth. She

spat it out, coughed, and tilted her head all the way back. It was the only angle she could now use to get a breath in.

Just go! I mentally roared. *Both of us don't need to be stuck here, and I'm the only one who doesn't need to breathe!*

"That hurt," she said in a hoarse voice, and then choked out a laugh. "Don't know how fish stand breathing that…"

She stopped speaking. I was terrified that she'd lost the remaining scant space she needed to breathe, and I couldn't angle my head in order to see. Her grip had loosened, and the currents from the incoming tide now had me facing away from her.

"This'll be weird," I thought I heard her say, and then her grip on me vanished completely.

Without it, I sank to the bottom of the cave. I tried to see where Denise was, but the green glow from my gaze barely cut through the water. Then, a tremendous thrashing turned my limited vision into nothing but movement and bubbles.

Pain ripped at me. That must be Denise, drowning. Oh, God, she'd suffer that horrible death over and over because she'd refused to leave me, and there was nothing I could do to help her! How many hours until low tide…?

A large shark suddenly filled my vision, mouth open as if grinning while it swam straight at me. Jesus, Mary, and Joseph! I'd never wanted to move so much in my life, but I could do nothing but stare as rows of knifelike teeth sank into my arm.

Agony shot through me, and inwardly, I screamed. In my darkest wonderings about how I'd die, and I'd had many of those, getting eaten by a shark had never made my list. Guess I hadn't given Fate enough credit. *Good one, you sick bitch!*

The shark bit me again, this time catching my upper shoulder. Amidst the new burst of pain, an image of the last time I had seen Bones flashed in my mind: his deep brown hair, creamy alabaster skin, high cheekbones, winged brows, full mouth, and eyes so dark brown they could have been black. And Katie, my beautiful little girl, standing next to him, watching me solemnly as I promised that I'd be back soon—

Red light suddenly suffused the shark's black eyes. Shock numbed me for a few seconds as to what that meant. In that short amount of time, the shark swam us out of the sacrificial chamber and into the cave's winding tunnels. There, its sleek body easily maneuvered around the bends and turns. I was the one who hit every protruding wall. Those hard jostles caused the shark's serrated teeth to tear deeper, but aside from holding me in its jaws, the shark didn't bite me again.

Red eyes. Only demons had those…or people whom demons had branded with their power, thus transferring some of their supernatural abilities to the branded person.

Jesus, Mary, and Joseph, I thought with awe this time. *You have outdone yourself, Denise!*

CHAPTER 6

If the shark's new red eyes weren't proof enough that this was Denise, the fact that it was carrying me out of the cave instead of eating me did. Sure, I knew that being branded by a shapeshifting demon years ago had given Denise the ability to transform into anything she wanted to, but I'd forgotten that anything meant, well, *anything*. I'd also forgotten that in many ways, the transformation was literal. Unlike the glamour used to cover the cave entrance, this wasn't a magical mirage. Denise didn't just look like a shark; she was one, as the water rushing through her gills and her toothy grip attested.

Don't know how fish stand breathing that, she'd said when she choked on the water, followed by a muttered, *this'll be weird.*

She must have realized the only way she'd get out of this unscathed was to breathe water like a fish, and not just any fish. The most badass fish in the sea. I might have been too heavy for her to carry before, but now? She glided us both through the waves like a hot knife through butter. If not for the searing pain in my shoulder, this would almost be fun.

In minutes, we were out of the cave. I expected Denise to drop me now that we were free of that labyrinth, but she kept swimming parallel to shore, adjusting her bite every so often when her many rows of teeth nearly severed my shoulder and almost sent me tumbling out of her mouth.

Each new bite had me mentally gritting me teeth. *How did you spend your girls' getaway, Cat? Oh, getting eaten by my best friend. No, not in the fun way. In the wow-that-hurts! way.*

I was starting to worry that Denise had taken her transformation a little too literally when she suddenly beached herself and spat me out with a painful rip. I lay there healing while the shark next to me shuddered several times before skin replaced scales and then Denise rose naked from the sand.

"Weird as fuck," she pronounced, spitting what was probably little bits of my flesh out of her mouth. "But it did the trick. There's the hotel, and unless I'm wrong, there's our cottage."

I had to take her word for it since I couldn't angle my head to look. Denise gave me a sympathetic glance, and then dragged me by the shoulders up the beach. I saw the steps of our cottage moments later, and then felt a hard thump from each of them as Denise dragged me up the stairs.

Once inside, she positioned me so I was sitting on the floor with my back braced against the couch. Then, she left my line of sight. Moments later, she was back, wearing a robe and a contemplative expression.

"Can you blink?" she asked me.

I tried and found that I could. She made a relieved noise.

"Okay, blink once for yes, twice for no."

I blinked once to show I understood.

"I saw a naked kid run out of what looked like a solid wall in the bluffs. He was cut up and screaming about witches and monsters, so I gave him my jacket, helped him up the incline, and told him to head for the hotel. While I was going back down, two women ran out of that 'solid' wall as well. So, I knew it was fake, and since you hadn't come out yet, I went in to find you. Were those women really witches?"

I blinked once.

"What about monsters? Were those real, too?"

I blinked twice.

"Guess that's good," she said in a weary tone. "So, if they were witches, a spell did this to you?"

I blinked once.

"Fuuuuck," she breathed out.

My thoughts exactly.

"I'll call Bones," she said.

I blinked twice in rapid succession. I couldn't wait to see him again after coming so close to death, but Bones wasn't an expert on magic, and we needed someone who was. Before I worried him halfway to his grave with my condition, I at least wanted some facts about it first.

Denise sighed. "I get it. You don't want him to see you like this until you know if it can be fixed."

I blinked once while fighting back tears.

Yes, exactly.

"Ian, then," she said. "Between him and Veritas, they've forgotten more magic than these witches probably ever learned in the first place."

I blinked once, hard. Yes, Bones's rebellious vampire sire, Ian, had been illegally practicing magic for centuries, and his several-millennia-old new wife, Veritas, was half-vampire, half demigod, so she almost had magic coming out of her pores.

Denise left. When she came back, she had her cell phone. "Calling and texting both of them now."

They must not have answered because she left two voicemails. Then, over the next few hours, she kept calling and leaving more voicemails and text messages. I was disappointed that she couldn't reach them, but I couldn't say I was shocked. Ian and Veritas had taken an extended honeymoon to parts unknown these past several months. Even Bones hadn't talked to them in a while, and he was Ian's only living family member.

"I'm sure they'll call back," Denise said, trying and failing to sound optimistic. She was married to a vampire, so she knew they didn't measure time the way humans did. It could take them days to check their messages, at least.

"In the meantime, let's get you cleaned up—"

"Don't bother."

The words came out of me, shocking us both. I'd thought them, but hadn't expected my mouth to form the words.

"Testing, one, two, three," I found myself saying.

Denise leapt forward and hugged me. "You can talk!"

"Seems so," I said, now trying to move, too. Still no motion in the limbs, but were my toes and fingers wiggling? With Denise blocking my view, I couldn't tell.

"Off," I said, and Denise jumped back.

"Sorry, did I hurt you?"

I could laugh, too, apparently. "Not then, but can we never play 'shark and chew toy' again, even if that was a great way to get us out of there?"

"Don't worry," she said, shuddering even though she was smiling. "It's been killing me not to leave you so I could brush my teeth, like, a thousand times."

I laughed again, and then gasped when I saw my hands and feet. Yes, my fingers and toes *were* moving. The spell was finally starting to wear off!

Denise's face suddenly drained of color, and she stared at something behind me.

"What?" I said, trying to turn around and failing. All I could do was crane my neck a little, and it wasn't enough to see what was behind me.

"Company," Denise said in a strained tone.

"Yes, company," an unknown female voice replied, followed by a wave of supernatural power that almost knocked me over even though I was still braced against the couch.

From the power stinging me like dozens of angry hornets, our "company" wasn't human, and she also wasn't alone.

Denise visibly tensed, but she planted her feet and didn't move. "All of you, don't come any closer."

"Begone, mortal," a new voice said, and Denise was suddenly yanked up by an invisible force and hurled out of the cottage.

I was strafed with broken glass before I tried and failed to stand. My feet and hands only made weird, jerking movements while the rest of my body stayed put.

Dammit, the spell wasn't wearing off fast enough!

"Don't get up," said yet another new voice, with an undercurrent that was more ominous than seeing how Denise had been magically swatted away as if she were a pesky fly. "I promise you that this won't take a moment."

CHAPTER 7

At least a dozen vampires wearing the same style of blue robes as the witches I'd killed earlier came into my line of sight. Good lord, of all the places to vacation in, we had to pick the one that was apparently a hotbed of witches!

One of the robed figures stepped forward and tilted her head. Her hood fell back, revealing hair the color of dark umber, deep brown eyes, and lovely sepia-and-cream skin.

"I am Morgana," she said.

"How unoriginal," I replied.

Okay, antagonizing a vampire witch while I was still mostly paralyzed wasn't my smartest move, but come on! Naming yourself after the sorceress who trapped the famed wizard Merlin from the King Arthur stories? She was asking for that sort of clapback.

Morgana glanced at my hands and feet with a smirk. "You must be very strong to have such motion. That spell doesn't expire until sunrise, but it matters not. Your death is sure."

I couldn't move enough to get away, but my hand worked well enough to give her my one-fingered opinion about that threat.

"Heard that from the other witches," I replied while focusing my energy on the silver knives I had stored in the bedroom. Even now, I was using my borrowed telekinetic ability to quietly pull back the zipper on the knapsack they were in.

Angry emerald light flashed in Morgana's eyes. "Do you have any idea what you did tonight?"

"Stopped an innocent kid from getting murdered," I said while thinking, *Keep talking. Your friend made that mistake, too.*

Now her brown gaze was all green, and fangs peeked out from her lips. "You interrupted a sacred ritual and killed seven of our newest coven sisters. Half of them weren't even vampires yet! Then, we had to sacrifice one of our sisters who survived your butchery because our goddess had already been summoned, and lifeblood is required after a summoning. At least our surviving sister gave us the means to avenge ourselves. We found you by following the magic in the spell they had left on you."

Some days, I really hated magic. Today was one of them.

"We'd kill you now, while you're still helpless," Morgana went on, almost hissing with rage, "but you don't deserve a quick, merciful death. So, we are giving you to our goddess."

With that, Morgana said something in an unknown language and drew her finger across my forehead. Everywhere she touched burned as if a hot poker was scorching me.

I quit being subtle and ripped open the satchel with my mind. Several silver knives flew out of the bedroom, but though they hit their targets, none of the vampires dropped the way they should have with silver in their hearts.

Morgana bared her fangs in a smile. "Before we had to sacrifice our coven sister in place of the boy you freed, she told us of your abilities. That's why we're wearing these."

With that, the vampires drew open their ceremonial robes to reveal that they were all wearing Kevlar vests. Murderous they might be, but dumb they were not.

Morgana traced my face with her finger again. This time, it didn't burn.

"Don't worry; you won't die tonight. I want you to think about what awaits you first. So, you have until the moon is full and the tide is high before our goddess comes for you."

I took it back—they *were* dumb. If they didn't kill me now, I would find a way out of this.

Morgana must have read some of that from my expression because she gave me a nasty smile. "Go ahead, let your loved ones gather around you trying to save you. You will only doom them, too. Everyone who spends so much as five minutes in your presence will be marked as a sacrifice, too, because this"—her finger traced my forehead—"is contagious. That's why we'll be leaving, but in case you're capable of surprising us with your abilities again…"

She said something else in that strange language. All of a sudden, I couldn't move a muscle. What had taken the other vampire several minutes with a supporting group chant to accomplish, Morgana had done by herself in seconds.

Maybe she'd chosen her name aptly after all.

The front door burst open, revealing Denise. She had cuts in several places and she was soaking wet…and furious.

"Back away from her, or I swear I will turn into a dragon and eat every last fucking one of you!"

The other vampires laughed. Morgana's brows rose, and she gave Denise an amused look.

"For the most entertaining threat I've heard in a while, you may live. For now," she added, with a sly glance at me.

I seethed, but I couldn't tell Denise to stay away from me. I couldn't so much as blink anymore.

Morgana gave me a final smile. Then, with a poof of smoke worthy of a B-grade horror movie, she and the other vampires disappeared.

Denise rushed over to me.

"Bitches knocked me all the way out to sea," she said while running her hands over me to check for injuries. "Sorry it took so long to get back. Are you hurt?"

I only stared, hoping that Morgana's threat was bogus. Maybe she'd only told me the mark was contagious because she wanted me to be too afraid to ask for help getting rid of it, assuming I could find a way to do that.

Denise made a sympathetic sound. "They hit you with another immobility spell, hmm?"

When I didn't blink or speak, she said, "Guess so. This one's stronger, if you can't even blink now."

God, what a cruel curse, forcing someone to be trapped in their own body while also dooming everyone around them. If I found a way out of this, I'd make those bitches pay.

"Something's on your forehead," Denise said, using the hem of her wet robe to wipe it. Then she frowned, rubbing harder.

"Sorry. It's not coming off."

No, it's not because it's a frigging contagious curse! I wanted to scream, but I could do nothing to warn her, and my helplessness burned more than the scorch of the mark.

Denise sighed and gave up trying to rub it off. "At least we know your paralysis is temporary, although it doesn't make sense that they'd find you, paralyze you again, and then *not* kill you. Yes, I threatened to eat them, but they don't know that I could really change into a dragon and do it."

Hope perked in me. *That's right, Denise, figure out that there's more going on here!*

"Something's up, isn't it?"

I stared at her as emphatically as I could.

"Thought so." She sounded resigned but not scared. "I'm calling Ian again. He can't ignore a ringing phone forever."

She spent the next ten minutes calling Ian and Veritas over and over. I swung back and forth between hope and terror as the time ticked by. Morgana had said anyone who spent more than five minutes in my presence would be cursed, too, but so far, Denise seemed fine. Maybe the witch *had* lied…

Denise suddenly dropped the phone. "I don't feel so good…"

Horror pierced me when a line appeared on her forehead. Then another one slowly snaked its way above her brows. Then another. Denise grabbed her forehead while, inwardly, I screamed.

No, no, no!

Denise walked toward the mirror above the bar, touching her forehead as her reflection showed more marks appearing. After a few steps, she staggered and almost fell.

No! I mentally roared again. *Please, God, no!*

"Shit," she murmured. "This is…bad, isn't it?"

Her words slurred, as if she were having trouble speaking. My God, it wasn't just the "sacrifice" curse that was contagious. The immobilization spell must have been, too!

And I could only watch, tears trickling out of my eyes. *Oh, Denise. I'm so, so sorry…*

She suddenly grabbed a bottle and a glass from the bar. Both almost fell from her hands, but she held on, and managed to spill some of the dark amber liquid into the glass.

What was she doing? I loved liquor as much as the next person, but this was hardly the time to drink!

She sank to her knees, yet one hand remained raised, holding up the glass. "Ashael," she rasped out, and then swallowed some of the liquor.

Ashael? The mostly not evil demon who was Veritas's brother? Sure, if anyone knew about magic, it was demons since their kind invented magic, but didn't demons require specific symbols drawn with virgin blood plus their true names in order to be summoned? That's the complicated ritual I'd had to do the one time I'd needed to summon a demon.

"Ashael, it's Denise," she went on, slurring her words so much that it was getting harder to understand her. "Come...*now*."

With that, Denise swallowed again. Then, the glass fell from her hand, and she collapsed onto the floor.

CHAPTER 8

I had to do something! Maybe I could use my powers to send out a text message to get Denise some help?

As quickly as that hope flared, it died. Even if I *could* use enough of my borrowed telekinesis to do that, anyone I called would be stricken by the contagious spell mere minutes after they got here. I might already have condemned Denise. I couldn't condemn anyone else—

Shadows suddenly swirled between me and Denise. In seconds, a tall, extravagantly handsome man with short black curls, deep brown skin, and walnut-colored eyes appeared. Never let it be said that demons failed to make a memorable entrance.

I stared at Ashael as he brushed imaginary lint from an expensive-looking peacock-blue suit. Then, red lit up his dark brown gaze as he glanced at Denise, at me, and then back at Denise.

"Got into a bit of trouble, haven't you?" he said with an appreciative whistle.

Denise groaned and sat up.

I was so shocked that I barely noticed Ashael pull out his cell phone and say, "Don't wait up," to whoever was on the line.

Had Ashael done something to Denise so she could move

again? If so, thank God! Or thank…whoever, since he was a demon.

"Whole…body's…stiff," Denise said with a moan.

Ashael's snort managed to be elegant. "Of course. From what I see, you've been doused with a powerful immobility spell. You wouldn't be able to move at all, except for those brands. Magic doesn't work on demons, and you have enough of our power in you to avoid being a living mannequin like your friend over there."

I wasn't even insulted. I was more stunned that Ashael knew that Denise was demon-branded. That was a closely guarded secret. Only me, Bones, Ian, Denise's husband Spade, and Denise's relative Nathanial knew about it, or so I'd thought. And how had Ashael known we'd been hit with a spell?

"Good thing both my natures protect me," Ashael went on. "Now I know why you sounded so desperate. Anyone else you called would only end up stricken by the contagion in that spell."

How could he know any of this? I mentally raged. *How?*

"Can you get…this spell…off us?" Denise ground out.

He paused. "Yes and no."

Always a bargain with demons, and those bargains rarely ended without a lot of regret on the bargainee's part.

Denise gave him a baleful look. "Do the…yes part."

Ashael came closer. "Are you sure? Neither of you will enjoy what it takes."

That sounded ominous. Maybe this wasn't a good idea.

Denise must have read my reluctance from my expression because she said, "Do me first, then."

Wait! That wasn't what I meant at all!

Ashael's lips twitched. "If only I had a dollar for every time I heard a woman say that…"

"You'd be rich?" Denise finished, managing an eye roll.

His grin widened. "Rich*er*."

With his sin-wrapped-in-seduction looks, I didn't doubt it, but that wasn't what grabbed my attention. It was the haze of light that now glowed from Ashael's hands, and how his gaze had gone from red highlights to twin beams of silver.

Holy shit. This must be Ashael's *other* side. I'd never seen it before, our previous contact being very brief, but I'd seen it from his half-sister, Veritas. And she'd almost leveled a house with that *otherness* after a mere mood swing.

"If you consent," he said to Denise while power thickened the air, "give me your hands."

Denise stretched out her hands. As soon as Ashael clasped them, that glow from his hands increased, and Denise screamed.

I didn't even have to concentrate. Every single bottle from the bar suddenly slammed into Ashael. Glass, alcohol, and then blood covered him from all the flying, cutting shards.

His gaze slanted my way in annoyance, but he didn't let go, and the glow from his hands only intensified. Denise screamed again, and then bit her lips as if to hold back another scream.

"I'm okay," she gritted out. "I know what he's doing."

Her words were no longer garbled from a half-paralyzed tongue. She also wasn't slouched over anymore. Now, she was sitting upright, even if her face was pinched with pain.

"How much more?" she asked with a gasp.

"Just a bit," he replied as more light poured from his hands. That light began to absorb into Denise's skin, until her whole body started to glow.

"Almost done," Ashael said in a soothing way.

White sparks came off their joined hands. Denise squeezed her eyes shut, breathing hard while the air filled with the strangest power. Not the skin-tingling energy that marked the auras of strong vampires, or the icy brushes of power that heralded grave magic. This was something I'd never felt before.

Ashael released her hands. Denise fell back. He caught her, lowering her to the floor across from where I was positioned. For a moment, our eyes met, and I stared at her in disbelief.

Were those flashes of *silver* in Denise's gaze now?

Then she blinked, and all I saw was Denise's normal hazel eyes. "Wow, that feels weird," she murmured.

With that, she stood up, moving as normally as she had before the spell had infected her.

Ashael scanned Denise and then nodded as if satisfied.

"That should hold you, but this power upload is only temporary. To make it permanent, we'd need to strike a deal, and despite what you know, I doubt you'd want to go that route."

"I don't," Denise said, adding "no offense," with a wry smile at him. Then, she glanced at me. "Don't worry, Cat. His power upload only hurts for a few minutes—"

"I'm not doing that with her," Ashael interrupted. "She has nothing in her to increase the way you did."

That sounded insulting, but more importantly, did it mean I was beyond help even from a half demon, half demigod like Ashael?

"I can, however, give her something to weaken the immobility spell so she can move again," he went on.

If my hands could have shot out to indicate consent, they would have. *Do it! Whatever it is, bring it on!*

"But she won't be good for much after that, and it's very important that you kill whoever hexed you both," he finished.

"Why won't Cat be good for much?" Denise asked, echoing my own thought.

His smile was as bright as sunshine. "She'll be too high."

I stared at the demon. Now I knew what he intended to give me to counter the spell. His blood.

Demons weren't just the inventors of magic; they were the walking embodiment of it. That's why spells didn't work on them. Their blood also had a unique effect on vampires, and by unique, I mean that vamps who drank demon blood ended up more wasted than a frat boy after a drinking contest.

Still, being wasted would be an improvement over my current

state. Besides, Ashael was only half demon. His other side was of an indeterminate celestial nature, so maybe his mixed blood wouldn't get me as trashed as straight demon blood would. Even if it did, Bones had once managed to win a fight to the death while sky-high on demon blood.

If he could do it, I could do it.

I stared at Denise, hoping she could intuit my answer.

She sighed. "I don't like this, but…Cat says yes."

Ashael rolled up his sleeve while grabbing one of the broken bottles I'd telekinetically hurled at him. Then, he came toward me with a wolfish smile.

"In that case, my lovely redhead, I hope you're thirsty."

CHAPTER 9

Being born half vampire meant that I'd only been drunk once, after a ghost had tricked me into chugging an entire bottle of uncut moonshine. Not even my half-vampire nature had been enough to make me immune to half a gallon of 180 proof "white lightning," as it turned out. Still, despite my relative inexperience with being intoxicated, I felt prepared to deal with the wonky side effects of Ashael's blood.

Oh, what a sweet summer child I was!

The first splash shot past my lips and went right down my throat. If my muscles still worked, I would've gagged.

Be a little more gentlemanly when shooting your load, Ashael!

At least I didn't need to worry about my lack of ability to swallow. With how forcefully his blood came out, it felt like it went straight into my stomach, and...wow, this rug was so thick. And *lush*. Had it always felt like this? And the colors in this room were so vivid, especially when reflected in the lights from all the broken glass.

"Beautiful," I sighed, and then squealed in delight.

I was talking again! Sure, I'd dribbled blood to say the words, but who cared? I wasn't wearing this dress again anyway.

"More," I said next, and grabbed Ashael's wrist.

"Uh, if she's moving now, is that enough?" Denise asked.

"No," I garbled out before Ashael could answer. Every swallow made the world more beautiful, warm, and glorious.

"Slow down, Cat," I heard Denise say.

I loved her, but she seriously needed to shut up.

Ashael's dark curls brushed my face as he bent near my ear. Even that slight touch felt like silk trailing over my skin.

"Last swallow, little vampire," he murmured, his voice curling around me like warm, dark waters.

"No," I said, my inhibitions drowned. "Eat you…all night."

Ashael's laugh was more decadent than the richest dessert. "If circumstances were different, I'd let you, but alas."

Then, his wrist was gone, and that addictive flow stopped.

I tried to yank his wrist back and ended up only grasping air. I leapt up to see Ashael on the other side of the room, wagging a finger at me.

"Ah ah ah, my lovely one. You're cut off."

I lunged at him, and then staggered in surprise when the floor rose up to trip me.

"Stop it," I snapped at the floor.

It undulated in response, taunting me. I stomped on it, and it surged up with an abrupt wave that knocked me flat.

Asshole.

Denise rushed over. "Cat! Are you okay?"

"Fine," I said, brushing her aside. This was between me and the floor, and I was kicking its polished driftwood *ass*.

I stomped up and down on it with all my strength. Planks cracked and gave way. When I was ankle-deep in the floor's wreckage, I howled in victory.

Take that, motherfucker!

"Cat…" Denise sounded worried, but she shouldn't be. I'd beaten the floor, so it couldn't attack her next.

"Don't bother trying to reason with her," Ashael said. "She's too high. Give her a few minutes to adjust to the effects of my blood. She'll be better by then."

"I'm fine," I told Ashael. "In fact, I'm *fabulous*."

His grin was annoying in its smugness. Should teach him a lesson. Make him bleed a little…and then lick it.

"She's, ah, growling," Denise said with concern.

Ashael waved. "Pay it no mind. Now, care to tell what happened that caused you two to run afoul of a sea god?"

"A sea god?" Denise repeated.

"You're both infected with contagious sea god magic, so you must have run afoul of one," Ashael said.

I was going to answer, but suddenly, the whole room tipped. Fucking floor was at it again! I grabbed the wall to stay upright, confused to see that Ashael and Denise were still standing without help. Why wasn't the floor attacking them, too?

Denise sighed. "I couldn't see most of what went down, but from what I know, Cat pissed off a bunch of witches, and they hit her with an immobility spell. They must have hit me with it, too, although mine didn't take effect until after they left."

"They didn't spell you. Cat did," Ashael said. At Denise's shocked look, he continued, "Not on purpose. You know I can see magic as easily as you see colors. That's how I saw that the magic on Cat is contagious. Once she was infected, she infected you. You would've infected me, too, if I wasn't a demon. This type of magic is very rare, so what did Cat do to anger those witches?"

"She stopped them from killing a kid," Denise said, sounding a bit dazed now.

Ashael whistled. "Ah. That'll do it. Ancient gods have *no* sense of humor when it comes to someone interfering with their sacrifices, and that child must have been the god's sacrifice."

"That's what they said," I filled in, no longer needing to hug the wall to stand. My head felt a little clearer, too, although I still thought the floor was daring me to a fight.

Ashael's dark gaze fixed on me. "That's why the sea god gave its acolytes the power to hex you with contagious magic."

"Goddess," I corrected him.

"Goddess, then. Did her acolytes tell you about the other spell they sealed onto you?"

"What other spell?" Denise asked, sounding surprised.

That's right, she didn't know. All of a sudden, I felt a lot more sober. "The one that makes me the goddess' new sacrifice on the full moon." Then, my voice hitched from more than the room-tilting effects of Ashael's blood as I added, "And anyone I've infected with the spell is her sacrifice, too."

"But you're a vampire," Denise sputtered. "Only decapitation or silver through the heart can kill you, and *nothing* can kill me except demon bone through both my eyes."

Ashael looked thoughtful. "Under normal circumstances, that's true, but with ancient gods, all bets are off. You have until the full moon, hmm? That gives you two nights."

"So, how do we kill this goddess?" Denise demanded.

Ashael snorted. "You don't. The sea is older than anything on this planet, so the gods it produced are among the most ancient and powerful. You can't kill her. Neither can I."

I started to speak, and then burped with such force that it rustled the hair around my face. I clapped a hand over my mouth, aghast. Then, despite our very serious circumstances, all of a sudden, I couldn't stop laughing.

"I haven't burped since I was human! Wow. That *sounded* like years of trapped air ripping out of me, didn't it?"

"There must be a way to stop this," Denise said, ignoring my comment.

Ashael gave her a level look. "Most spells die with their caster, so kill the witch that hexed Cat, and that should do it. I warn you, though: a witch powerful enough to channel sea-god magic won't die easily, and my race has a truce with other gods, so I can't help you. The sea goddess would consider my killing her acolytes a violation of that truce. But vampires and humans have no such truce, so as long as you offer the sea goddess a substitutional sacrifice, she shouldn't avenge her acolytes if you kill them to break the spells."

Really? That was some bullshit.

"Bad goddess," I said.

Denise didn't seem to care about the sea goddess's refusal to avenge her acolytes. "How do we find the witch who hexed Cat in order to kill her?"

I waved my arms. "I know this one! The same way they tracked me, through the magic in their spell. Right?"

Ashael inclined his head. "That, I could do for you, but aside from that, and from leaving you more of my blood to stave off Cat's immobility spell, I must remain out of this."

"You've already done so much," Denise said, touching his shoulder. "I don't know how to thank you."

Ashael's smile was half sardonic, half wistful. "You already did when you and your husband claimed me as family last year. You both had reason to hate demons, and Veritas had only demanded you show me respect, yet you called me family while expecting nothing in return." He touched the hand she'd placed on his shoulder. "You don't know how rare that is, but I do."

"I meant it," Denise said softly.

He gave her hand a light squeeze. "I know. It's why I came at once when you called."

"Aww," I said, coming over to them. "So sweet. Group hug!"

Denise let me hug her, but Ashael teleported away right as I got close enough to snap my fangs at his neck.

"Too slow," he said, laughing as I cursed him in frustration. "And too obvious. You need to be much stealthier if you're trying to steal some of *my* blood."

Denise gave me a cagey look, and then turned to Ashael. "How long before your blood stops giving her immunity from the immobilization spell?"

He rubbed his jaw. "A few hours, probably. That's why I'll leave more blood for you. She'll need it so you can get her somewhere safe before you go after the witch who hexed her and, by extension, you."

"Denise isn't doing that alone," I protested.

Ashael's brows rose. "You think you can help her in your condition?"

"Fuck yeah," I said, incensed at the scorn in his voice.

"Cat." Denise's carefully neutral tone made me swing around to stare at her. "Maybe it's better if you sit this one out."

She didn't think I could help either? Doubt frothed up, covering my anger. Were they right?

Was I…useless again?

Fuck that! "Come at me," I said to Ashael, decision made. "No demon tricks. You'll play the evil vampire witch, I'll be me, and if you stop me from skewering you through the heart with silver, I'll stay behind."

Ashael sighed. "You can't fight. You can barely stand—"

"Then this won't take long." I waved at him in the universal gesture for 'bring it on.'

Ashael just stood there and stared at me.

"Lazy demon," I muttered, and charged him.

He sidestepped with an ease that made me so angry, I didn't notice the wall until I hit it. Then, a smack on the back of my head gave me another face full of plaster. When I spun around, Ashael was studying his nails as if his swat hadn't given me a second face plant into the now-dented wall.

"We finished?" he asked in a light tone.

Anger burned like someone had detonated a flare inside me. "Not nearly."

I charged him again, this time swerving into his sidestep. His overconfidence cost him, and I landed a punch that rocked his head back. When I went for another, he pivoted and swept my legs out from under me. My head cracked against the floor as I fell, hard.

Dammit! I should've anticipated the leg sweep. That was Fighting 101, and I'd fallen for it. I was still too sloppy, and he was taking full advantage, as any opponent would.

Ashael's sigh as he stood over me stung more than my hitting the floor had. "I'm only fighting as if I'm a mere vampire, and you're still unable to best me. Stop now, Cat. This is getting embarrassing."

Rage briefly cleared the fog in my head. I'd been trained by the toughest, dirtiest fighter in the vampire world! Drunk and sloppy I might be, but I was *not* going down this easily.

I got up and lunged at him, not fighting my sloppiness this time. He saw it and went for the leg sweep again. Right before I reached him, I dropped low and slid beneath his kick while punching his other knee with everything I had.

It fractured with an audible crack. At once, I yanked at his still uplifted leg, throwing him off balance. His broken knee crumbled when his weight shifted onto it, and he crashed down on top of me hard enough for me to briefly see stars.

No problem. I didn't need to see. All I had to do was think. *Now, knife! Now!*

An instant later, I felt a thud as something hit Ashael's back. Denise gasped, and Ashael rolled onto his side, showing the knife handle now sticking out of his back. Thank God my fledgling telekinesis wasn't sloppy drunk like the rest of me.

"Who's embarrassed now?" I ground out.

Ashael threw back his head and laughed.

"By the gods, even high, you're as vicious as you are beautiful. Are you certain you love your husband, my feisty little redhead? You and I could have such fun."

His voice deepened until it felt like an acoustic caress at that last word.

I got up with a snort. "Not a chance, and believe me, I have *plenty* of fun. Bones isn't just my husband's name, it's practically his life motto."

"TMI," Denise muttered, but Ashael laughed again.

"Then I'll take my defeat with grace, if I must."

He vanished, leaving the knife to land on the floor now that it no longer had a back to stick into. The blade was still coated with his blood, and I'd snatched it and licked it before it occurred to me how crass I was being. Then, I didn't care as his blood lit my senses up even more.

Oh, that felt so good!

"Should I be worried about her new…enthusiasm for demon blood?" Denise asked Ashael when he reappeared next to her.

"Only if she seeks it out after you've defeated the witches," Ashael replied. "Otherwise, this is only a temporary craving while she's under the influence, although I strongly advise that you don't let her drive."

Denise gave him a look that said, *Do you think I'm stupid?*

Ashael grinned before his expression became serious.

"I'll return later with more blood, and later again once I've found your witches. In the meantime, let Cat teach you how to fight. You have powerful abilities, but those witches have powerful magic, so if you're going to survive, you need more than your shapeshifting skills."

"I can fight," Denise sputtered.

"Done!" I said with a jaunty wave at Ashael.

He nodded at me, and then vanished with a swirl of shadows that were much more impressive than the witches' smoke trick.

Denise sighed and then turned to me. "There's too many people who could get close enough for us to infect them if we stay here, so we need to leave."

I nodded, trying to ignore how the simple gesture made the room swim. I'd felt much more focused while fighting with Ashael, but that must have been rage combined with muscle memory from all my years of fighting. Now, however, I felt downright woozy. Had that little amount of blood I'd licked off the knife made me so much worse? Or was I truly feeling how high I was, now that I didn't have anything left to prove?

Either way, Denise was right. We had to leave before we infected anyone else.

"Yes, and once we're somewhere safe, I'm going to turn you into a world-class ass-kicker."

CHAPTER 10

Okay, so I might have been overambitious when I said I could turn Denise into a world-class fighter. Even under the best of circumstances, doing that in less than two days would be hard. Trying to do that while supernaturally sloshed? That was next to impossible.

It wasn't easy on Denise, either. Imagine trying to learn to fight from a sky-high teacher. If Denise took a shot every time I said "See what I did there? *Don't* do that," I wouldn't be the only one so intoxicated that I had to incorporate tripping into our fighting routine.

Still, we muddled through, after we found an Airbnb cottage up the coast near Dogtown; an unincorporated community in Marin County that used to be called Woodville. The place lacked every amenity we'd enjoyed at the Ritz's beach house, and that was fine. It also lacked neighbors for at least a mile in every direction. The population of Dogtown was only thirty people, so the owner was all too happy to make the unexpected reservation, even at that pre-dawn hour.

The small, one-bedroom cottage had a fine layer of dust over the scant furnishings, plus the only scents I caught were must and mildew, but its neglect suited me. No one being here recently meant that no one would come into contact with our contagious magic. Also on the plus side, the little cottage had a flat yard bordered by the nearby forest. That's where I trained Denise until I felt a lot more sober, which coincided with it being harder for me to move as the effects of Ashael's blood wore off.

Denise helped me back into the house. I could still walk, but if I thought I was staggering before, it was nothing compared to how my muscles were seizing up now.

"Put me on the couch," I said. "You take the bed. You need the sleep, and it won't matter where I am once I freeze up."

She gave me a pitying look, though thankfully, she didn't argue. She just helped me onto the sofa.

"I'll put your knives and your phone next to you," she said, and briefly disappeared into the bedroom. When she came back, she set my knapsack near my feet.

"Thanks. I want to use my cell to record a message, while I can still speak enough to do it."

Her expression clouded as she sat next to me. "You're recording a message for Bones?"

"Yeah," was all I said.

She was silent. Then, she said, "I suppose I should do the same for Spade," in a tone much thicker from emotion.

I felt so awful, it took me a moment to reply. "I'm sorry, Denise. If I hadn't gone after that scent of blood—"

"Then you wouldn't be the person who saved my life the night we met," she interrupted, her tone turning hard despite her eyes brightening with unshed tears. "If you remember, a vampire was turning my neck into an all-you-could-eat buffet. You heard my scream, came running, killed him, and saved me. So no, I won't let you apologize for saving that boy tonight, either. Saving people is what you *do*, and I'm glad because I wouldn't be here now if it wasn't."

Now I was the one fighting back tears. "I was the lucky one that night. Your friendship has saved me so many times."

"Metaphorically, maybe," Denise allowed, with a little smile. "Especially when you were so miserable while you were hiding from Bones. But that wasn't the only time you saved my life. You also did it when a horde of zombie-like things attacked that New Year's Eve, and you did it when a vampire drug dealer was trying to turn me into his latest sellable product."

"I wasn't alone any of those other times," I protested.

She took my hand. "You're not alone now either, Cat."

My throat closed up. Not from the spell overcoming me. From all the emotions welling up to take away my voice.

"Thank you," I finally managed to say.

She squeezed my hand. "You're welcome."

We sat in silence for a few minutes. Then she said, "You shouldn't just leave a recorded message. You should call Bones."

Oh, how I wanted to! I'd give anything to hear his voice right now, but if I did, I knew how it would end.

"I can't. No matter how I pretend, Bones will know something's wrong, and if he knows that, he'll track me down. Then, he'll get infected, too. I can't let him do that. If things go south, one of us needs to be there for Katie."

Denise gave me a sad smile. "That's why I'm not calling Spade. He'd insist on coming, too. We don't have a child to worry about raising, but regardless, I don't want him getting infected. Ashael's power upgrade to my demon brands might protect me from the immobilization spell, but I'm still marked as a sea goddess sacrifice, and I'm still contagious, too."

I squeezed her hand. "We'll kill the witch who hexed us. That'll reverse both spells, and we'll both be okay."

She squeezed back. "I know we will. And, hey, in the meantime," her tone brightened, "I get to learn how to fight. I've wanted to do that for years, but Spade kept brushing me off when I'd ask him to teach me."

"Why?" Her husband was notoriously overprotective, and the vampire world was frequently violent. Because of both, I would've thought Spade would be all over teaching Denise how to defend herself if she asked him.

"I think he…took it personally." Denise sounded bemused. "Like I was implying that he wasn't doing a good job protecting me when it wasn't that at all. I wanted to learn how to fight for *me*. It had nothing to do with him or his abilities."

I found myself scrunching into a smaller shape even though it was hard for me to move. Wow. This was hitting close to home.

"Well, you're learning now," I said while wondering if I owed Katie an apology for how I might have misinterpreted her reasons for training. "And you'll learn again tomorrow, once Ashael drops off more blood."

Denise rose. "Speaking of that, I'll go summon him so he knows where we are. I'll do it outside so you have some privacy while you record your message for Bones."

She left, taking a bottle and a glass with her. I waited until I couldn't hear her anymore, and then I placed my cell in front of me and hit *record*.

Or I tried to. It took two attempts before I pressed the right button. I didn't have long before I froze up like a mythical gargoyle turning to stone in the sunlight.

"Hey, Bones," I said when it was finally recording. Then, I forced a smile. "If you're watching this, things didn't go as planned, but I want you to know that I love you. So, so much. That's why I couldn't tell you what happened until now…"

Fifteen minutes later, Denise returned. I was still recording, but I'd stopped speaking. I couldn't talk anymore. I couldn't even move to shut off the phone. At least I'd said what needed to be said, even if it felt woefully inadequate. The truth was, I'd never be ready to say goodbye to Bones, even if I had over a thousand years with him. And Katie…How did you begin to say goodbye to your child?

Denise shut off the recording. Then, she swung my legs up over the side of the couch until I was lying on it instead of sitting. Finally, she tucked a blanket over me.

"Ashael didn't answer, but I'm sure he'll be here soon. In the meantime, try to sleep. There's nothing else to do anyway."

There wasn't at the moment, but I doubted I'd sleep. I had too much on my mind.

We just have to kill one vampire, and this will be over, I reminded myself. *Just one. Easy-peasy.*

Except this vampire was also a powerful witch, so it wouldn't be easy. She also probably wouldn't be alone, so we'd have more than her to contend with. Plus, we had no guarantee that killing her would nullify our spells. Ashael had said that it should. What he didn't say—what he couldn't say—was that it *would*. Sometimes, killing the spellcaster didn't end a spell. Only the spell's completion did, and our spells would only be complete when we were sacrificed to the sea goddess.

"You know what I'm going to do, once this is over and we've won?" Denise said in an admirably confident tone. "I'm going to start the adoption process."

If I had any movement, my eyes would have widened. Denise must have sensed my surprise because she let out a soft laugh.

"I know, I didn't tell you that Spade and I have been talking about adopting. It was too serious to discuss over the phone, and I was still undecided. Sure, I could technically have a baby since I still get my period, but Spade's sperm has been dead for centuries, and I didn't want to go the in vitro route. I'm demon-branded. What if the kid came out with demon-y powers? Or I miscarried because I accidentally shapeshifted in my sleep? I did that once, you know. I blame you because I was thinking about you when I went to sleep. Then, a few hours later, Spade woke up to a friggin' *cat* in his bed."

I couldn't laugh out loud, but on the inside, I was wheezing with humor. Poor Spade, and poor Denise! Aside from the obvious issue of suddenly waking up as another species, Denise was also allergic to cats.

"So, no pregnancy for me," she went on. "But I always did want to be a mom, so why not adopt?"

Why not, indeed? She'd make a wonderful mother, and Spade would be a great dad, though he'd probably spoil his kid rotten.

I'm so happy for you, Denise, and we will win tomorrow, I wanted to say. *We have so much to live for. No murdering, sea-hag-worshipping bitch is going to take that away from us.*

Shadows suddenly leapt from the corners before stretching into the familiar form of a tall, startlingly handsome man. Ashael wasn't wearing a suit this time. He was in a fluffy white robe and nothing else, as a breeze revealed when it lifted a corner of his short robe.

"Sorry for the delay," he said. "I didn't expect your summons so soon."

"Sorry if we caught you, ah, entertaining," Denise replied. That's when I noticed the lipstick marks on his neck. Guess he wasn't in a robe because we'd disturbed him from his bath.

He waived. "They'll wait."

They. So, not just one. No wonder he'd taken more than half an hour to respond.

"I brought you more blood," he said, pulling two bags out and handing them to Denise. "Give one to her before training tomorrow, and the other when you leave to meet the witches, but you'll need to hide the second one until then."

As if I would risk our lives by stealing it early! Then again, no sense trusting the willpower of someone trashed. After all, I'd licked a knife coated in his blood mere hours ago.

"I've also found some of the witches," Ashael said, snapping my attention back to him. "They appear to be prepping for a special ritual. There are several covens in one place, yet thus far, I haven't seen the one you described as Morgana."

Bad news on top of more bad news. Our luck this trip

wouldn't have it any other way. We couldn't attack until we knew Morgana was there. She was the spellcaster, so she was the one we *had* to kill.

"But don't worry," Ashael went on. "If Morgana is as high-ranking among the coven as you suspect, she wouldn't be involved in the preparations. Royalty never sullies itself with menial labor. She'd wait until the end to appear."

Plausible. Morgana hadn't been at the sea cave, either. Guess some events really were too lowbrow for her. At least this ritual sounded important, if it had multiple covens. She should show up for the end of that.

"Remember, once you attack, any new spells the witches hurl at you shouldn't fully stick while the power in your brands is increased, Denise," Ashael continued. "They also should mostly bounce off Cat because she'll be so newly filled with my blood. The witches won't expect that, so be sure to use it to your advantage."

"Oh, we will," Denise said, and took the new blood bags with a glint in her eyes that I hadn't seen from her before. Sure, I'd seen that same look from many dangerous opponents in the past, and it had doubtlessly been in my own eyes several times, too. It was the look of anticipated violence.

"So, where do we crash this ritual?"

Ashael smiled. "Check your phone. I sent you a pin."

CHAPTER 11

"Watch where you're going!" Denise said for the third time.

If I didn't love her, I'd be annoyed. Had I flown us into the cliff face yet? No, so she should quit bitching. Sure, I'd come close to the rock walls to our left, but that was because we were being stealthy as we approached the rendezvous point.

Normally, you needed to hike almost seven miles to reach Alamere Falls. But I could fly, so we were arriving the easy way. Or, at least, it *would* be easy, if Denise didn't keep screeching in my ear and distracting me.

I had to give it to the witches; they'd picked a beautiful place for their ritual. The forty-foot falls landed on Wildcat Beach, where the surf was rapidly covering the sand as the tide started to come in. At this hour, no tourists were around since it was already a tough hike to Alamere Falls during the day.

It was only an hour before high tide on the full moon, when the second spell would kick in and the sea goddess would come for us. We were cutting it close, not that we'd had a choice. The witches hadn't been here earlier. I'd done multiple fly-bys and hadn't seen a hint of them. I'd started to worry that they'd concealed themselves with glamour—or that I was too drunk to spot them—when I finally saw a line of blue-robed figures hiking up the final stretch of trail leading to the falls. I tried to do a quick head count, and lost track after the mid-twenties. Whatever. I only needed to find and kill Morgana. She had to be here. This was the big shebang. Morgana wouldn't miss it.

I flew back to where I had left Denise, drank the last of Ashael's blood from the mostly empty second bag, and flew us back to the falls. Time to crash their party.

The witches were setting up a bonfire made of branches and the terrain's many loose rocks. No one had removed their hoods yet, so I couldn't spot Morgana's lustrous, dark umber hair.

Come on, Morgana. Where are you?

"Look!" one of them suddenly said while pointing up.

Dammit. We'd been spotted.

"Brace!" I told Denise as every hooded head looked up.

I dove us toward the tightest cluster of witches. We'd scatter them before landing near the bonfire—*Aw, shit!*

I crashed into the bonfire. Fire, wood, and stone burst out in every direction as we tumbled along the top of the cliff. Thankfully, a group of witches stopped our momentum, providing a much softer landing than the ground as we plowed into them.

I leapt up with as much bravado as I could muster after that epic fail of a landing.

"Give me Morgana, or I am going to fuck all of you!"

Denise shot an amazed look my way. That's when I realized I'd forgotten a very important word.

"*Up*," I stressed. "Give me Morgana, or I am going to fuck all of you *up*."

"Your first offer was better," an amused voice noted.

I knew that voice. Morgana.

I turned and flung several of my silver throwing knives toward the source of her voice. *Take that, witchzilla!*

The knives turned to liquid in midair before splashing to the ground near her feet. Worse, I suddenly felt a burning wetness, and looked down to see silver rivulets running from my now empty weapon sheaths on my arms, thighs, and ankles.

I stared at the shiny splotches in disbelief. *Please let me be hallucinating from Ashael's blood. Please don't let the bitch have just melted all my weapons!*

Morgana smiled. "How do you like my new spell?"

Oh, I'd be very impressed, if I wasn't the one covered in useless, melted silver. "Creative," I managed to say.

Morgana's smile turned smug. "I had a feeling you'd find a way out of the immobility spell, so I had that ready in case you showed up tonight."

"Cat..." Denise drew my name out in a concerned way.

I glanced over at her. Yep, Denise now had melted shiny streaks where all her silver weapons had been, too. Ashael had said his blood would shield us from any new spells they lobbed our way, but that protection obviously didn't extend to inanimate objects like our knives.

"It's fine," I said, cracking my knuckles. "Who doesn't love a good old-fashioned brawl?"

"Alas, I must decline," Morgana replied in a light tone. "We have our goddess' arrival to prepare for."

A high-pitched scream sounded behind me. I turned, seeing a brown-haired boy struggling between several witches. Freckles or pimples dotted his face, and his frame had that awkward, bones-too-big-for-his-skin look that some teens had. When his eyes met mine, horror, shock, and fear practically spilled from his gaze and his thoughts were a jumble of pleas and shrieks.

Firecrackers of rage went off inside me. "Another kid? What the fuck is wrong with you? If the goddess you worship *must* have a living sacrifice, chose a murderer or a pedophile like a normal person!"

"That's what I said," one of the nearby witches muttered, garnering her an instant censoring look from Morgana.

"We hold to the old ways of offering a pure sacrifice—"

My loud scoff cut her off. "First of all, you're evil. Second, purity is a spiritual state, not a sexual one, and third, wow are you dating yourself as an old, out-of-touch vampire if you think 'teenager' automatically means 'virgin.'"

"I'm done speaking with you," Morgana said, and picked up one of the sticks from the now-destroyed bonfire. Then, she poked it at a splotch of melted silver near her feet.

"I couldn't agree more," I spat and marched toward her, throwing aside the witches who tried to stand in my way.

Morgana didn't move. Instead, she threw the stick at me.

I didn't even duck. What was this, kindergarten?

The stick changed into a large snake that hit me right in the mouth. I flung it off, yelping in a very un-badass way, but I hated snakes, and now I'd just gotten to first base with one.

"Really?" I snapped when dozens of other branches suddenly morphed into serpentine life. Now, I had a field of snakes between me and Morgana. Gross, but did she actually think this would stop me from reaching her—

Ouch! One of the snakes bit me, and wow, it hurt. A lot.

I yanked the snake off, not caring that I ripped my flesh in the process. Its fangs were still oozing venom, only it wasn't normal-looking venom. It was shiny and metallic.

"Silver," I breathed out.

A single touch confirmed it. Only silver stung that much. All vampires were allergic to it, even freaky former half-breeds like me. Worse, liquid silver couldn't be removed with the same ease as yanking out a weapon, and until the silver was removed, I'd be weaker and I wouldn't heal as fast.

I hurled the snake aside. "Magic snakes? You need therapy!"

Morgana only tossed her hair. "And you need to sit quietly until our goddess comes to claim you, but I'm guessing neither of us is going to do what's in our best interest, are we?"

Denise grabbed my arm. "You okay?"

The bite in my calf burned like hell, but I'd be all right. I just needed to keep from getting bitten again.

"Fine," I said through gritted teeth. "Hold the other witches back while I kill her, will you?"

Denise dropped my arm and backed away a few feet.

"With pleasure."

I rose into the air, a little more wobbly than usual, but at least the snakes couldn't bite me up here.

"You're dead," I said to Morgana, and flew at her.

She shot upward right before I reached her, leaving me to plow into the spot where she'd stood. After I spat out a face full of dirt, I saw her flying in a graceful circle above me.

"I don't think so," she said in a pleasant tone.

Bitch could fly. She was also creative, powerful, and beautiful. If I weren't straight, married, and repulsed by child murderers, I might have developed a crush.

"Fellow coven sisters." Morgana raised her voice. "Teach this impudent vampire to show me the proper respect!"

The witches grabbed the magic snakes and hurled them at me. I flew up, avoiding most of them, but at least two sets of fangs sank home. That deadly silver venom scalded me from the inside out. I tumbled out of the sky, hitting the rapidly disappearing beach hard enough to scatter sand in every direction.

I staggered to my feet, cursing when I tried to fly and couldn't. Fucking liquid silver was weakening me by the moment, and only massive cutting could remove it. I'd do it, too, if I had any weapons, but thanks to Morgana, I didn't.

Screw it. I'd fight without flying *and* weapons, then.

"I warned you, motherfuckers!" I heard Denise yell.

Poor Denise, stuck up there with dozens of murderous witches and God-knew-how-many magically venomous snakes. I had to get to her. Right now.

I started climbing up the cliff wall. Jagged rocks sliced up my hands, making my grip slippery from blood. I didn't care. All that mattered was killing Morgana.

The cliff suddenly shuddered while large rocks struck my head and bashed into my body. The heavy barrage made me lose my grip. I stopped my fall by shoving my hand into a crevice hard enough to shatter bones. Pain screamed through me, but now I was anchored to the cliff wall, and I ducked beneath the next onslaught of rocks.

What was this? An earthquake? We were in California; it was possible. Or was this more of the witch's tricks?

My bet was on the witch. "Is that all you've got, Morgana?" I shouted. "If so, I'm still coming for you!"

No answer except screaming. Hmm. That didn't sound like Denise. Instead, it sounded like several of the witches.

Another blast of rocks pelted me, and the cliff wall next to me crumpled before sliding off onto the beach. Shit, maybe this *was* an earthquake. I crab-crawled away from the growing hole, avoiding the worst of the landslide. Then, I raced toward the top as fast as I could. Two minutes later, I heaved myself over the still shuddering ledge…and stared.

I'm hallucinating. Wow. Ashael's blood is good shit.

A grayish-green dragon stomped after a group of witches. Every step from the massive beast made the ground tremble, and its thick, whiplike tail swept aside the snakes that tried to swarm it. When one of the witches got too close to its flank, a huge wing snapped out and flattened her.

Another witch grabbed a snake and hurled it at the dragon. The viper latched onto the dragon's neck while thin, shiny drops rolled down its thick scales as the snake tried to pump its magically derived venom into the beast.

The dragon's roar blasted the hair back from the nearby witches. Then, its head snapped out with surprising speed. For a second, all I saw was the bottom halves of the witches' blue robes because the dragon's thick head blocked the rest of them. Then, the dragon reared back up, clenching several big, blue, bloody forms between its teeth.

That's when I realized I wasn't hallucinating.

Back away from her, or I swear I will turn into a dragon and eat every last fucking one of you! Denise had said two days ago. *Morgana and the others had laughed, but no one was laughing now.*

Except me.

"Ha ha ha ha! Oh, it's *on* now, bitches!"

CHAPTER 12

Morgana tried to fly away. Denise swatted her back to the ground with one of those massive wings. Morgana rolled around, momentarily dazed, and I seized my chance.

I jumped on her. She tried to scramble away, but I climbed up her body with the same urgency I'd used to scale the cliff.

"I take it back," I said when I had crawled near her ear. "You don't need therapy. You need killing."

Morgana started screaming in that unfamiliar language. Instantly, it felt like dozens of invisible nails scratched me. Nothing else happened, though, and from Morgana's shocked expression, something more should have.

I laughed. "Nice try, but I've got friends in low, *low* places, so I'm temporarily immune to your spells."

She glared at me. "You will die screaming—"

My arm across her throat cut her off. I folded my other one over it, locking her neck in place between them. Then, I wrapped my legs around her torso and began pulling.

Her eyes widened, first in rage, and then in horrified understanding. She flung herself backward, knocking us against the ground hard enough to elicit an *oof!* from me, but I didn't let go. I kept tightening my grip and pulling harder.

"Morgana!" one of the witches screamed, seeing her leader's predicament. She ran toward her, only to be snatched up before she was halfway there. Several crunching sounds later, there was nothing left of the witch except the parts that Denise spat out.

Morgana's elbows slammed into my sides. Pain exploded as my ribs shattered. Every new movement caused ragged bits of bone to stab me, and I wasn't healing. I was too full of silver.

My arm slipped a bit from her neck. Morgana took advantage, rolling us across the ground while ramming her elbows into me again. Soon, I was vomiting blood between gasping screams, yet I didn't let go. I let her bash me while I readjusted my grip on her neck and kept my legs around her torso.

It's only pain. Keep pulling! Harder, harder, harder!

Morgana's head came off with a pop that sent me sprawling backward. Then I sat there, so dazed from agony that it took a few moments before I chucked her head aside. It rolled to a stop near her body, which was now shriveling into the state of true death for vampires. Soon, Morgana looked like a weird headless scarecrow that someone had dressed up in a bloody blue robe.

I lay back, relief briefly buffering my pain. It was over. Morgana was dead.

A roar made me sit up despite how much that hurt. Denise had chased a group of witches over to the cliff's edge. They had a steep drop behind them and a pissed-off dragon in front of them. They might have deserved either death, but I was eager to get the silver out of me so I could start healing, and I'd need Denise in her regular form for that.

"Enough," I called out. "Morgana's dead, so you can stop. Not you, witches," I added when they froze as if obeying a sternly worded command. "Denise, *you* can stop."

She did stop advancing on them, but the witches didn't move. Huh. Maybe they were literally scared stiff…or not.

I sat up more fully and looked around.

Now none of the witches were moving, even the ones that had been running down the path away from the edge of the cliff.

"The spell," I groaned.

As promised, it had infected everyone in our immediate vicinity. How ironic that the witches had gotten trapped in a hex of their own making. Still, that hex was supposed to end with Morgana's death, and the witches were freezing up *now*, after Morgana was dead.

Only one reason I could think of, and it was the worst possible scenario. Morgana's death hadn't ended the curse.

"She comes!" one of the witches suddenly screamed.

I thought she meant Denise, but she was still in her imposing stance in front of the cliff. The witches perched at the cliff's edge tried to turn around toward the sea and couldn't. They did manage to crane their necks a little though, so I stood up and followed the direction of their gaze.

The sea boiled. That's the only way I could describe the froth of white that poured from the tops of the waves. Then those white tips began to spin in a circle, forming a maelstrom that slowly approached the thin strip of remaining beach.

High tide was here. The sea goddess was coming, and Denise and I were still magically marked as her sacrifices. But we weren't the only ones. Not anymore.

"New plan!" I yelled, striding toward the witches even though every movement caused fresh spurts of agony. "Any witch that can still move better conjure something up to break Morgana's spell, or we're *all* about to be sea goddess chum."

"Blas…phemy," the witch nearest to me hissed.

Her broken speech concerned me more than her refusal. It meant the immobility spell had almost completed its work. The witches around her looked in equally bad shape. They must have been the closest to us since we'd arrived. They couldn't chant out a counterspell even if they wanted to.

I gave a frustrated look around. *Someone* had to be in better shape! We hadn't been up in every witch's face this entire time.

I heard a thump behind me and then gasps. I turned, shocked to see that the witch who'd said "blasphemy" would now never speak again, and it wasn't because of the spell. No, it was because her head was rolling near my feet while the rest of her body was still frozen upright.

"Who else wants to tell my wife that they won't help her?" a completely unexpected British voice said.

CHAPTER 13

I swung around. Nope, I wasn't hallucinating this, either. Somehow, Bones was about fifty yards away from me and closing fast. Spade was behind him, moving slower because he had a canon-like object strapped to his back, multiple ammunition belts crisscrossed over his torso, and two mega-sized machine guns in his hands.

"Darling," Spade said as his spiky black hair blew around his pale, handsome features. "Love your new look."

Denise's expression was so openly shocked that I needed to get a picture. "Ooh, who's got a cell phone handy? A dragon making that face would be the *perfect* meme!"

Bones and Spade exchanged a look.

"She's even drunker than we are," Spade muttered.

Drunker than…huh?

Belatedly, it struck me that Spade's normally aristocratic tones were now distinctly slurred, and Bones swayed a touch as he strode toward me. I also hadn't felt them approach and they were Master vampires with auras that crackled the air around them with their power, so I *should've* felt them.

Unless they'd both dropped out of thin air.

"That devious demon!" I said, exasperated.

Ashael knew that Denise and I weren't involving our husbands while we were contagious, but had he respected our wishes? No, he'd teleported them here himself. At least it looked like he'd pumped them full of his blood first.

Bones flashed his fangs in something too feral to be a smile. "Exactly what I said when I learned he'd known of your predicament for days, but that's off-topic. What's on-topic"—he raised his voice—"is that if anyone wants to leave here alive, you *will* remove the hex from these women now."

"Or I will hunt down and slaughter everyone you love after I finish murdering you in the most painful way possible," Spade added in the coldest of tones.

"That's dark," I muttered while as a chorus of witches spoke. Unfortunately, most of what they said was barely intelligible from their broken speech. My teeth ground.

"They can't chant away a curse in their condition even if they wanted to, and since they're now marked as sacrifices, too, most probably *do* want to. But that immobility spell is hella effective. Did you-know-who leave you any extra blood?"

"No," Bones said before stopping mid-stride and turning to the nearest mostly frozen witch. He ripped his wrist open with a fang and held it to her lips.

"Drink," he said harshly.

Her eyes widened, but with Bones willing his blood into her mouth, she had no choice except to swallow.

Spade saw that and swung one of his guns over his shoulder. Then, he grabbed the witch nearest to him and fed her some of his demon-fortified blood, too.

"Now, start undoing this curse," Bones ordered.

Both witches started to chant in clear, unbroken voices. That's right, we could share our version of spell-buffering through our demon-altered blood. I immediately opened my wrist and held it over the mouth of the witch next to me.

She swallowed twice before her eyes widened and she fell over.

"Sil...ver," she gasped out before her eyes rolled back in her head and she spasmed as if I'd stabbed her.

Aw, shit! My blood was now vampire poison thanks to those damned silver-venom snakes. I'd probably be on the ground next to this witch, if not for all the demon blood I'd consumed. Guess I was too high to feel all the damage done to me, even though what I did feel was brutal enough.

A sharp whistling sound went off behind me, like a train barreling down the tracks. When I turned, sea spray was swirling so high in the air that it had reached the top of the cliff. It looked like a water spout, if one of those could trail a waterfall behind it like a cape. But this was no natural phenomenon. The sea goddess had reached the top of the cliff.

Suddenly, my silver poisoning was the least of my problems.

"You need to leave," I told Bones, swinging back around. "You and Spade have already been exposed to us for too long. If you don't go now, you'll end up marked as sacrifices, too."

"Not a bloody chance," Bones snarled. "And if any of these bitches want to survive the next five minutes, they'll undo your hex *right now* or they'll get this."

Another witch suddenly lost her head. I might not have mastered my telekinesis yet, but Bones was surgical with his abilities, if that surgeon was homicidally pissed.

"Wait, we can do it!" the witch Bones had given his blood to said. "Most of us never wanted to sacrifice kids anyway. We wanted to go after murderers or pedophiles like she said!"

"How...dare," another witch rasped. "We honor...old ways."

"Times change," said the witch Spade had given blood to. "I want to live long enough to change with them."

"Wise choice," Bones ground out. "Now, point to the most powerful among you, and be sure to pick those with good survival instincts because if they cross me, you'll eat your own heart."

The witch pointed, and Bones and Spade began giving more of their blood to the witches she'd indicated. At the same time, the dragon abruptly deflated like it was no more than a very elaborate balloon. Then, Denise rose up naked from the remnants of her leftover scales.

Spade yanked the robe off the witch he was giving his blood to, revealing that she was wearing jeans and a Miley Cyrus shirt under it. Then, he gave Denise her robe. She put it on, grabbed the next witch, and ripped her wrist across the witch's fangs.

"No!" Spade said as Denise's demon-branded blood spurted into the witch's mouth. Only Ashael's blood would have been more potent, and one taste gave away the source of Denise's powers. It also marked Denise as a vampire's version of a walking drug.

The witch's eyes widened as she swallowed. Then, she sucked at Denise's wrist as if she were starving. When Denise yanked her arm away, the witch howled, "Wait! I need more!"

"No more. Now, chant away that hex with the rest of them," Bones said in a steely tone.

The witch kept screeching for more…until her arm tore free and her own hand reared back and slapped her in the face.

"I said *chant!*" Bones roared.

Even high, being slapped with her own dismembered limb was enough to scare the witch into complying. She began to chant.

Denise shook her head. "Okay, I should give less of my blood to the next witch," she said under her breath.

That aquatic tornado came closer. I tried to back away and suddenly found that I couldn't. *What?* This wasn't the immobility spell acting up again. I could move closer to the writhing, spinning waterspout. I just couldn't move away from it.

Denise abruptly stopped giving blood to the other mostly frozen witches, and from her expression, she hadn't wanted to. Then, the markings on Denise's forehead started to glow at the same time that my own forehead began to burn.

"Cat?" Denise said, her widened hazel eyes meeting mine.

I wanted to scream. I also wanted to hurl every weapon ever created at the towering funnel of water coming ever closer, and I couldn't. I could do nothing at all. Despite my best efforts, I'd lost and I wasn't the only one about to pay the price.

Tears made everything blurry. "I'm so sorry, Denise."

Why couldn't it just be me? Why did it have to be her, too? *I'd gone after the witches! She'd done nothing to deserve this!*

Bones was suddenly in front of me, blocking my view of the approaching sea goddess. He picked me up, but when he tried to carry me away, he couldn't budge me despite his feet digging furrows into the ground from his efforts. Then, his power flared until my skin burned from the residual energy and still, I didn't move a fraction. Whatever magic that marked me as her sacrifice now anchored me to her path despite Bones pitting all his physical and telekinetic strength against it.

I might not have been able to leave, but he could.

"Bones, you have to go *now*."

I couldn't let him die, too. I'd rather be fed to that watery monstrosity a thousand times than be the cause of that.

"Please go. Please," I said, and shoved at him with all my strength. "You can't let her take you, too."

"She's not getting either of us," he snarled.

I wished that were true, but I could only save one of us.

"It's okay." I forced back every screaming emotion enough to crease my face into a smile. "A little thing like death can't separate us. Not in any way that truly matters, so be the father that Katie needs and *leave*."

My voice rose on that last word, riding on the tears that I refused to shed. I wouldn't let his last memory be of me crying. In so many ways, I had nothing to cry about. I'd been so, so, so lucky. I'd had more love than I had ever dared to wish for, and I'd take the memory of that with me wherever I went.

His arms only tightened around me while he kept me locked out of his emotions.

"I *am* being the father Katie needs. That's why I'm not letting this waterlogged bitch take her mother." Then, he raised his voice. "If either one of them dies, every last one of you will beg for a merciful end, so bloody well chant!"

The witches' voices rose until their desperation was clear even if I couldn't understand what they were saying. Then, all I heard was a barrage of gunfire followed by a series of booms that shook the ground hard enough to make cracks appear.

Spade was unleashing his arsenal.

"No one stops chanting!" Bones shouted above the din.

Over his shoulder, I saw the waterspout part and then fall away like a discarded cape. In its place was a seven-foot-tall mostly humanoid woman. Frothy seafoam trailed from her head, reminding me of the Bible verse "it leaves a glistening wake behind, as if the deep had white hair." Her skin was the color of moonlight on water; not blue, not silvery white, but changing between each color with every glance. And her face…I shuddered even as I fought the urge to kneel.

Her face was the very essence of the sea; in one moment stunningly beautiful, and the next pitilessly violent.

The witches' chants grew until they were louder than the gunfire that had no effect on the sea goddess. Spade may as well have been firing his rounds into the deepest part of the ocean. When the gunfire stopped and all I heard was several futile clicking sounds, I knew Spade had run out of bullets.

He let out an anguished roar. Then, an assault rifle hurtled toward the sea goddess. It passed through her and disappeared over the cliff. Somehow, that got her attention better than all the bullets had because the swirling twin maelstroms in her face that marked her eyes now settled on Spade.

"No!" Denise shouted. "Leave, Spade. Hurry!"

"Like hell," he snarled, his voice sounding closer. "Wherever you go, I go." Then, "Crispin, you know what to do."

The sea goddess came closer, flowing over the ground like a river rushing over stones. The markings on my forehead that denoted me as her sacrifice kept burning as if they'd been set on fire. I knew it was useless, but I tried to back away again and didn't gain so much as an inch.

"Last chance!" Bones shouted, his power flashing out in rolling waves that made screams briefly interrupt the witches' chants. Then, the witches began shouting a single word so loudly that my whole head rang from the sound.

"*Ustap.*"

The goddess looked away from Spade to focus her strange, swirling eyes on me. I shoved at Bones, begging him to leave. He only flared his power out again. The witches' shouts grew louder, until the ground trembled from them. Still, the goddess didn't look away from me. Then her arm rose, water falling from her fingers, as she reached for me—

"*Ustap, ustap, ustap!*"

The pain in my forehead stopped with the same abruptness that her arm dropped. Then, she recoiled from me as if I were foul. All of a sudden, I was moving, too, my surroundings blurring from speed as Bones flew us away.

CHAPTER 14

"They did it!" I heard Spade shout, followed by Denise's glad cry. Then, I heard nothing except the wind whistling by as I saw the ground fall away and grow smaller.

Bones must have decided that flying us in the opposite direction wasn't enough. Now, he was flying us up and away, too.

For a few blissful seconds, I didn't care. All I focused on was the feel of his arms around me, the sweet sting of his hair whipping against my cheek, and his scent, like crème brûlée combined with the finest whiskeys. I didn't even feel pain from the silver or my many unhealed injuries. I was too happy.

At last, we were free. All of us.

Well…not all of us. Ashael had said if we broke the curse, the sea goddess would require a substitutional sacrifice for me and Denise. Morgana had mentioned the same. *We had to sacrifice the sister who survived your butchery because our goddess had already been summoned, and lifeblood is required after a summoning.*

The freckled boy's face flashed in my mind. He was still there, and the sea goddess still needed at least two sacrifices to make up for the ones she'd lost, assuming that Spade had rushed Denise away as soon as she could move, too—and he would have. That meant we'd left a helpless kid alone with a bunch of witches who'd shown no hesitation when it came to murdering innocents to appease their goddess.

"Bones, we have to go back," I said.

Either he couldn't hear me, or he was ignoring me because he didn't slow a bit.

"We have to go back," I repeated louder, punching his arm for emphasis. "There's a kid back there they're going to kill!"

That earned me a truly impressive curse, but he did do an aerial version of a U-turn. Soon, I saw the battered, half-collapsed side of Alamere Falls again.

The witches were still there, blue robes fluttering as they scurried about to rebuild the bonfire. That's all I saw before Bones headed toward the lower part of the trail further down from the bluffs. Once there, he landed, let me go, and then zoomed back up while I yelled at him not to leave me there.

He ignored me. Soon, I couldn't see him at all, and now I was a few miles away from the cliff.

"No, you don't," I growled as I ran up the trail.

Each movement felt like evil pixies were stabbing me inside, but I didn't slow down. Injured or no, I wasn't staying behind. The curse was off me now, so I was in no more danger from the sea goddess than Bones. He'd refused to let me face her alone earlier. I'd be damned if I let him do that now.

Still, it took several aching minutes to climb to the top of the trail, and I passed more than a few robed, headless bodies along the way. From how they were still in the process of shriveling, these looked like very recent deaths. Apparently, Bones had decided to make an entrance.

I was about to skirt by them when I heard frantic thoughts about staying hidden combined with a rapid heartbeat in the bushes to my right. Most of the witches had been vampires, but there had been a few humans among them. I yanked the thickest part of the bushes aside, and found myself staring into wide, panicked brown eyes.

"Don't hurt me!" the freckled boy wailed.

Thank God that he was still alive, and he'd had the presence of mind to hide, too.

"Good job," I told him.

His eyes darted in every direction, reminding me of a panicked horse. "Stay back. You stay away from me!"

I was anxious to get to Bones, but I couldn't leave the kid like this. He had every reason to be freaked out. He'd seen things tonight *I* hadn't seen before, and I'd seen a lot. That's why I didn't bother telling him to trust me (he wouldn't) or to calm down (in his state, he couldn't.) Instead, I fired up the glow in my gaze and put all the power I had left into my voice.

"You're okay now," I said in the resonating tone all vampires had. "You partied with the wrong girls tonight, and they slipped you drugs that made you hallucinate some wild stuff, but you'll be fine."

"Wrong girls…wild stuff," he repeated in the dazed way of a human under vampiric control.

"Yes, but none of it was real," I said, still holding his gaze. "It was just the drugs. Now, you're safe, and you'll be going home soon, so you're not afraid anymore. But for a little while, you're going to close your eyes and stay right here."

"Stay right here," he repeated, shutting his eyes.

Good. Now, he'd be calm and stay put until I could come back to get him. I put the thickest part of the bush back in place, concealing him again, and resumed my trek.

By the time I reached the top of the bluff, the bonfire was lit, the sea goddess was swaying in front of it, and Bones was emitting so much supernatural energy that approaching him felt like walking into an electrical storm.

"I don't care which ones you sacrifice, so hurry it up," he

snapped to a black-haired witch with high cheekbones and tawny skin.

I recognized her as the first witch who'd agreed to undo the hex, and I was struck with an idea.

"Don't pick just any witches," I said. "Point out all of Morgana's cronies that supported her child sacrifices. If the rest of you really want to change your coven's ways, now's your chance."

"No!" screamed a forty-something year old witch with parchment-pale skin and iron-colored hair.

I grunted. "Guess we know which side you were on."

Several witches tried to run. Bones's power flashed out, stopping them faster than the immobility spell. Then, his power reeled them back toward the sea goddess, who let out a noise that must've been the watery underworld's version of "nummy, nummy."

"That one, too," the pretty black-haired witch said, pointing at a witch that was trying to nonchalantly back away toward the trail. "And that one. Her, too."

When she was done, Bones held eight witches in front of the sea goddess, far more than the "substitutional" requirement to replace me, Denise, and the kid. Wow, she'd feast tonight.

A hard thump suddenly sounded to my left. I jumped until I saw that it was only Spade, Denise in his arms, landing near the edge of the bluff.

"Not finished yet, Crispin?" he asked, calling Bones by his human name as he always did.

"Almost, Charles," Bones replied, doing the same. Bones might have chosen his vampire name after rising in a shallow graveyard full of exposed bones, but Spade had chosen his as a reminder that he'd once been referred to only by the tool his prison overseer had assigned him: a spade.

"Quiet," said the dark-haired witch. "We're about to begin."

I didn't want to watch this, but I didn't trust them enough *not* to watch, so I stayed where I was and shut my mouth.

The eight sacrificial witches didn't. They screamed out threats that abruptly ended when Bones froze their lips as well as their bodies. That made it easy for the dark-haired witch to trace those burning patterns onto their foreheads, marking them as sacrifices. When she was done, she stepped back and the sea goddess surged forward. Then the goddess passed her hand over them, giving each a single touch, before backing away.

That was it? It hardly looked lethal—

The witches suddenly collapsed. In the split second it took them to fall to the ground, they had all turned into water, leaving only multiple splashes to hit the rocks instead of their bodies. The splashes were quickly absorbed into the sea goddess, until the former eight witches were nothing more than another sheen of liquid on her glistening form. Then she, too, turned into water that splashed back down the cliff and into the waiting sea.

I would've been less disturbed if she'd opened her mouth and eaten them whole. That, at least, would have left the witches *who they were*. But she'd reduced them to nothing at all, in less time than it took to blink, and the reality of that hit me like a brick to the head.

That could have been me and Denise. It was *supposed* to be us, and the sea goddess had been reaching for me right before the spell broke. She'd come so close to touching me…

Rage exploded through my subconscious, almost knocking me flat as Bones's shields cracked and his emotions burst through. Clearly, I wasn't the only one thinking about how close I'd come to being a splash on the ground that the goddess absorbed.

Then, that door slammed shut, and I only heard his fury as he said, "You were going to do this to my wife."

Death dripped from every word. The black-haired witch trembled as she backed away.

"We had no choice," she said in a hoarse tone. "You saw how powerful Morgana was. She ruled us for over four hundred years! Anyone who challenged her was fed to the goddess—"

"Oh, you'll wish for such a quick death," Bones said as his power cracked, whiplike, through the air.

Her eyes bulged and her neck stretched to an impossible length. So did all the other witches' necks, until they all resembled taffy being pulled by a machine.

"Stop!" I cried out.

Bones swung an amazed look my way. "Why? They meant this for you and Denise. They *did* this to who knows how many young lads, so they all deserve to die."

"They do, but then none of them will be left to tell other covens like theirs that the sacrifice of innocents stops now," I said in as strong a tone as I could manage. I wasn't sure how much longer I could speak, let alone stand, so I had to make this count. "We found this group through their magic. In the same way, we can find the others, too, so they all need to know that we'll be checking up on them to make sure that covens only sacrifice the worst of the worst of humanity from now on."

Bones's face was set in hard, unreadable planes, but for an instant, his shields cracked again, and I felt admiration threading through his vengeance-fueled rage. He recognized the logic of letting them live to warn the others about changing their ways even though he really, really wanted to kill them.

"Very well." If death had dripped from his other words, now reluctance coated his tone. "With these terms, you may live."

The witches' necks stopped stretching. The ones that were vampires recovered in a few seconds, but the few humans among them dropped to the ground, dead. Then, the black-haired witch gave a solemn nod first at me, and then at Bones.

"We'll do things differently from now on, and we'll make sure that we're not the only coven, or you won't have to find the others through magic because I'll tell you where they are."

With that, a cloud of smoke poofed out. In the moments it took to clear, all of the witches had disappeared. Even their dead were now gone, and I blinked in disbelief.

"If they had the ability to teleport themselves out of here, why didn't they leave before now?"

"Because that's not teleportation," drawled a familiar voice.

No one had been sitting on the edge of the makeshift stone bonfire seconds ago. Now, Ashael perched there as comfortably as if he were getting ready to toast some marshmallows.

"That's a parlor trick," he went on. "It stuns the senses for a few seconds so it *looks* as if they've teleported away when in reality, they scurried out of here as fast as they could run. Still, it takes a bit of doing to momentarily daze vampire senses. Before they absorbed residual power from their goddess' feeding, they couldn't have pulled off such a trick."

That explained why they hadn't done it before, but I got why they did it now. "Fake" teleportation or no, it had still worked in getting them out of here before Bones changed his mind about letting them live.

"Ashael." Bones said his name as if it tasted sour. "Been loitering about, watching this whole time, have you?"

"Of course not," Ashael said with mock indignation. "My presence would have violated my race's treaty with the other gods. I would never do that, just as I would never add a dollop of magic to the witches' hex-dissolving-spell because the silly birds couldn't conjure up enough power to do it on their own."

My jaw dropped. *Ashael* had topped off the witches' undoing spell in time to save us?

Denise ran across the bluffs and threw her arms around him. "You beautiful, beautiful demon!" she choked out.

Ashael laughed as he patted her back. "I am, but as I said, I would never do such a thing. That's against the rules, and an obedient fellow like me *always* follows the rules."

"Of course you do," Denise said, laughing as she pulled away. "My mistake."

Ashael winked at her, and then held out a tiny glass bottle to me. "Drink this before they cut the silver out of you. It'll help."

I grimaced. "Thanks, but if that's more of your blood—"

Ashael was gone before I finished the sentence. Bones and Spade exchanged a look, and then Bones flew over to the stone bonfire and plucked the bottle off its ledge.

"Not blood," he said after pulling out the stopper and sniffing the bottle's contents. "Smells like flowers."

It could smell like fresh manure, and I'd still drink it if it wasn't more demon blood. Nothing against their kind, but I'd had enough of being high. Still, maybe I'd be lucky and Ashael had brought me the vampire version of Novocaine. If so, I'd never forget his birthday, assuming demons celebrated birthdays.

"If this stuff makes me pass out, or if the silver extraction does, the kid that the witches brought here is down the path in the bushes," I said. "He's bruised, but otherwise fine, and I gave him a new memory of what happened tonight."

"We'll see him home safely," Spade said. "Now, let Crispin tend to you. You look ghastly, Cat."

I let out a pained huff. "Thanks."

"Cat."

Denise came over and knelt in front of me. She didn't speak, and neither did I. We just stared at each other, and then we started to laugh because otherwise, we might have cried. We'd both been through so much these past few days that it would take time to fully process everything. All I knew right now was that I had the best friend in the world. Oh, and that I'd never forget *this* girls' getaway.

"Same time next year?" I quipped.

"Over my dead body," Spade muttered, but Denise laughed again.

"Sure, only next time, *I* pick the location and venue."

"Deal," I said and hugged her, ignoring her protest that she didn't want to hurt me.

"Everything's at maximum pain anyway, so don't worry."

"Speaking of that." Bones knelt next to me. "We need to get that silver out of you, luv. Want to try Ashael's potion first?"

I took the bottle and downed it. It tasted like rosewater and I didn't feel high, so Bones was right: it wasn't more demon blood. Hmm. Wonder what it was and how it was supposed to help. So far, I didn't feel anything...

Hey, I didn't feel *anything*. I poked myself in the ribs, which should have doubled me over since most of them still hadn't healed, but all I felt was the give where my finger pressed in.

"It's the magical version of anesthesia," I said with relief. "I can't feel anything, so go ahead and cut away."

Bones's cell phone started vibrating. So did Spade's. Bones ignored his, but Spade pulled his cell out and glanced at it. Then, he let out a sardonic grunt.

"It's Ian, texting over and over to say something's wrong with Cat and Denise, and to call him at once."

"It took him *three days* to listen to our messages?" Denise shook her head. "Remind me not to call him in an emergency again."

I only laughed. Sure, I'd almost died, plus I had a gruesome supernatural surgery in front of me, but now that I was free of pain, free of a deadly spell, free of the fear that I'd doomed my best friend, and free to go home with the man I loved, I was in the best mood ever.

"Yeah, well, better late than never, right?"

EPILOGUE

Three days later, I walked through the woods bordering our house in the southwestern-most part of Canada. Pine needles crunched beneath my feet, announcing my presence well before Katie could see me through the thick trees, but this time, I wanted her to hear me approach. I was done spying on her.

"Hey," I said when I reached the clearing where she was.

Katie's shoulders hunched ever so slightly as she glanced at the felled trees around her before meeting my eyes. They hadn't fallen from natural means, which would be obvious even if I hadn't known what she had been doing out here.

"Hi."

She sounded unsure, which wasn't like her. Katie normally had the poise of someone three times her age, which was another reminder of how her childhood had been robbed from her.

I nudged one of the fallen saplings with my foot. "Clean break all the way through. One kick did it, huh?"

"You know?" Katie whispered, turning a shade paler.

"Yeah, honey," I said softly. "I know. I'm not mad at you, either. I just want to know why you were hiding it from me."

She didn't say anything for several moments. I waited,

schooling my features not to show anything except love and acceptance. I needed her to know that she could tell me anything, no matter what it was because nothing would ever, ever make me stop loving her.

"I didn't want you to see me this way," she finally mumbled while looking at her feet instead of me.

"What way?" I asked as gently as I could.

"The way I looked when I killed people."

Now she looked up at me, and her dark gray eyes contained more pain than any child's gaze should have.

"I never used to think about them, but now, I see them in my dreams, and it isn't like before because now I *care*."

Her voice rose at that last word, and if her speech had been carefully measured before, now she rushed through what she said as if she couldn't get it out fast enough.

"I only saw them as targets before. Messy ones because of all the blood, but just targets. So, when they begged, it was only noise, and when they died, I was glad because that meant I'd passed the test, and they were only *targets and tests* to me back then. But now, I know they were people who wanted to live, and I remember what they said when they begged me, and I know what I took from them when they died because now, I love people, too, and I want to take back what I did but I *can't*."

My eyes burned and my throat felt like a hot coal was stuck in it, but I refused to cry. This wasn't about me. It was about Katie, and I needed to let her get all of this out because there was so much more here than I'd realized.

"You're not to blame for their deaths," I said, my voice a little hoarse from the emotions I was holding back. "The people who turned you into a weapon are. You didn't know any better because you were only a child. They *did* know better and they used you anyway, so they're the real murderers. Not you."

Katie swiped a hand across her eyes, catching the single tear that had fallen. Then, she nodded sharply.

"Most days, I understand this. But then I see them in my dreams, and it brings it all back. Training is the only thing that makes them go away, so I keep coming out here to train."

My poor little girl! How she'd suffered, and worse, she'd suffered alone even though I'd been right there the whole time.

"How does training make them go away?" I asked, squelching my need to hug her and tell her I'd make it all better. I had to let her talk. She'd carried this inside her long enough.

"Because they know I'm doing this for them," she said, gesturing at the pile of felled trees. "I can't take back what I've done, but I'm going to make sure I'm strong enough and fast enough to stop other people from hurting those like them in the future. So, instead of being the weapon that kills people who need help, I'll be the person who saves them. Like you."

Like...me?

That was it; I was going to ugly cry. There would be rivers of snot. I might never recover from it. But first...

"Just be who you are." My voice was husky because that lump in my throat felt like it had detonated. "Not who you think you should be. Who you are is enough, Katie. It will *always* be enough. And you don't have to hide your training from me anymore. You don't have to hide any part of yourself, ever. I love all of you, and I always will. In fact, if you want to"—I shifted positions until I was in a classic fighting stance—"I'll even train with you. If you're going to do this, let's make it a little fun."

Katie's eyes had shone, hearing the first part of what I'd said, but at my training offer, her gaze clouded with skepticism.

"Thank you," she said, now sounding almost comically polite. "But I don't know if that would be a good idea. I'm a very skilled fighter. I don't want to hurt you."

I almost burst out laughing in addition to still wanting to cry myself into a state of snotasia. Oh, she had a *lot* to learn. First was that I'd always love her and be there for her, no matter what. Second was that her mama might not be able to cook, sew, or hold a conversation without dropping at least one f-bomb, but she could fight until the cows came home.

Or, at least tonight, I could fight until Bones finished with dinner in about an hour.

"Come on, sweetie," I said, circling her while I cracked my knuckles and rolled my head around my shoulders to loosen up. "*This* is what your mama does best."

The End

THE OTHER HALF OF THE GRAVE

From *New York Times* bestselling author of the Night Huntress series, Jeaniene Frost, a dark and sexy new look at the iconic origin story of Cat and Bones, as experienced by Bones…from the other half of the grave.

There are two sides to every story – and the sizzling British alpha vampire, Bones, has a lot to say…

Out on 4/26/22
Order at your retailer of choice!

ALSO BY JEANIENE FROST

Author's Note: The Night Rebel, Night Huntress, Night Prince and Night Huntress World series all contain stories set in the same paranormal universe. The Broken Destiny series is set in a different paranormal universe that's unrelated to those series. Thanks and happy reading!

– Jeaniene Frost

Night Huntress series (Cat and Bones):

Halfway to the Grave

One Foot in the Grave

At Grave's End

Destined for an Early Grave

One for The Money (ebook novelette)

This Side of the Grave

One Grave at a Time

Home for the Holidays (Ebook Novella)

Up From the Grave

Outtakes from the Grave (Deleted Scenes and Alternate Versions Anthology)

A Grave Girls' Getaway (Novella in The Hex on The Beach anthology)

Night Huntress World novels:

First Drop of Crimson (Spade and Denise)

Eternal Kiss of Darkness (Mencheres and Kira)

Night Prince series: (Vlad and Leila):

Once Burned

Twice Tempted

Bound by Flames

Into the Fire

Night Rebel series (Ian and Veritas):

Shades of Wicked

Wicked Bite

Wicked All Night

Broken Destiny series (Ivy and Adrian)

The Beautiful Ashes

The Sweetest Burn

The Brightest Embers

Other Works:

Pack (A Werewolf Novelette)

Night's Darkest Embrace (Paranormal Romance Novella)

ABOUT THE AUTHOR

Jeaniene Frost is a *New York Times* and *USA Today* bestselling author of paranormal romance and urban fantasy. Her works include the Night Huntress series, the Night Prince series, the Broken Destiny series, and the new Night Rebel series. Jeaniene's novels have also appeared on the Publishers Weekly, Wall Street Journal, ABA Indiebound, and international bestseller lists. Foreign rights for Jeaniene's novels have sold to twenty different countries.

Jeaniene lives in Florida with her husband Matthew, who long ago accepted that she rarely cooks and always sleeps in on the weekends. In addition to being a writer, Jeaniene also enjoys reading, writing, poetry, watching movies, exploring old cemeteries, spelunking and traveling – by car. Airplanes, children, and cook books frighten her.

Jeaniene loves hearing from readers and you can find her on her website (https://www.jeanienefrost.com/) or socials:

Twitter twitter.com/Jeaniene_Frost

Goodreads goodreads.com/author/show/669810.Jeaniene_Frost

YouTube https://www.youtube.com/user/JeanieneFrost

Printed in Great Britain
by Amazon

47421830R00056